CHILDREN OF ARAMAR

JOS

Sonia Moruno

CHILDREN OF ARAMAR

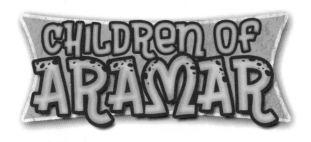

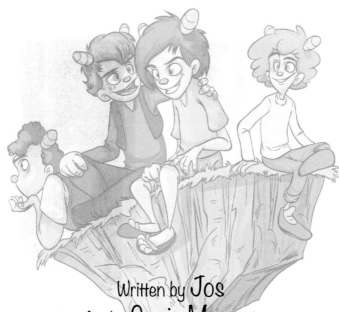

Written by Jos

Art by Sonia Moruno

Translation by Anna Rosenwong

Letters by Frank Cvetkovic

Edits by Justin Eisinger and Alonzo Simon

Design by Gilberto Lazcano

For international rights, contact licensing@idwpublishing.com

ISBN: 978-1-68405-502-9

22 21 20 19 1 2 3 4

IDW®
www.IDWPUBLISHING.com

Chris Ryall, President & Publisher/CCO • **John Barber**, Editor-in-Chief • **Cara Morrison**, Chief Financial Officer • **Matthew Ruzicka**, Chief Accounting Officer • **David Hedgecock**, Associate Publisher • **Jerry Bennington**, VP of New Product Development • **Lorelei Bunjes**, VP of Digital Services • **Justin Eisinger**, Editorial Director, Graphic Novels and Collections • **Eric Moss**, Sr. Director, Licensing & Business Development

Ted Adams and Robbie Robbins, IDW Founders

Facebook: **facebook.com/idwpublishing** • Twitter: **@idwpublishing** • YouTube: **youtube.com/idwpublishing**
Tumblr: **tumblr.idwpublishing.com** • Instagram: **instagram.com/idwpublishing**

Originally published by Ediciones Babylon as LOS HIJOS DE ARAMAR.

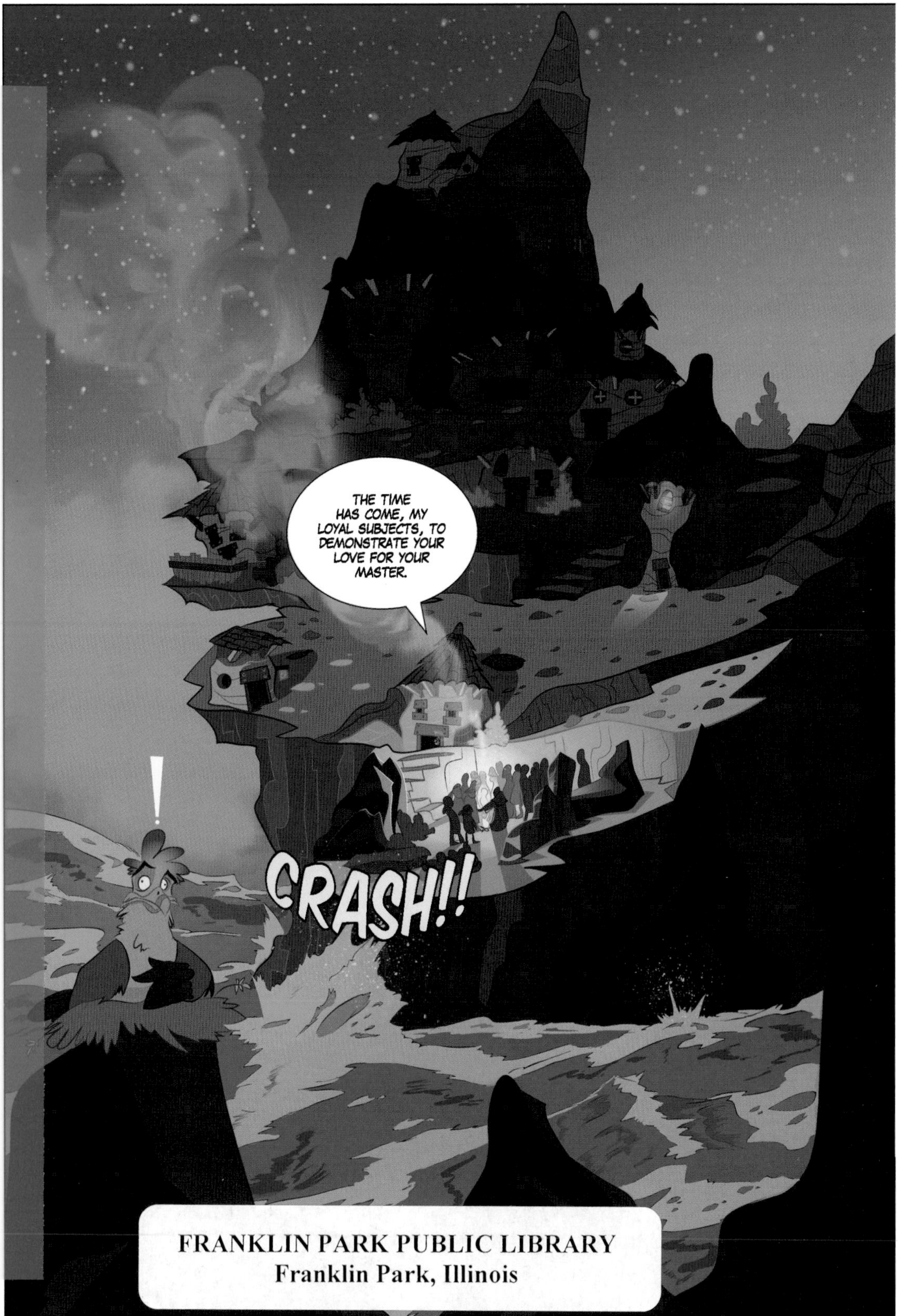
THE TIME HAS COME, MY LOYAL SUBJECTS, TO DEMONSTRATE YOUR LOVE FOR YOUR MASTER.
!
CRASH!!

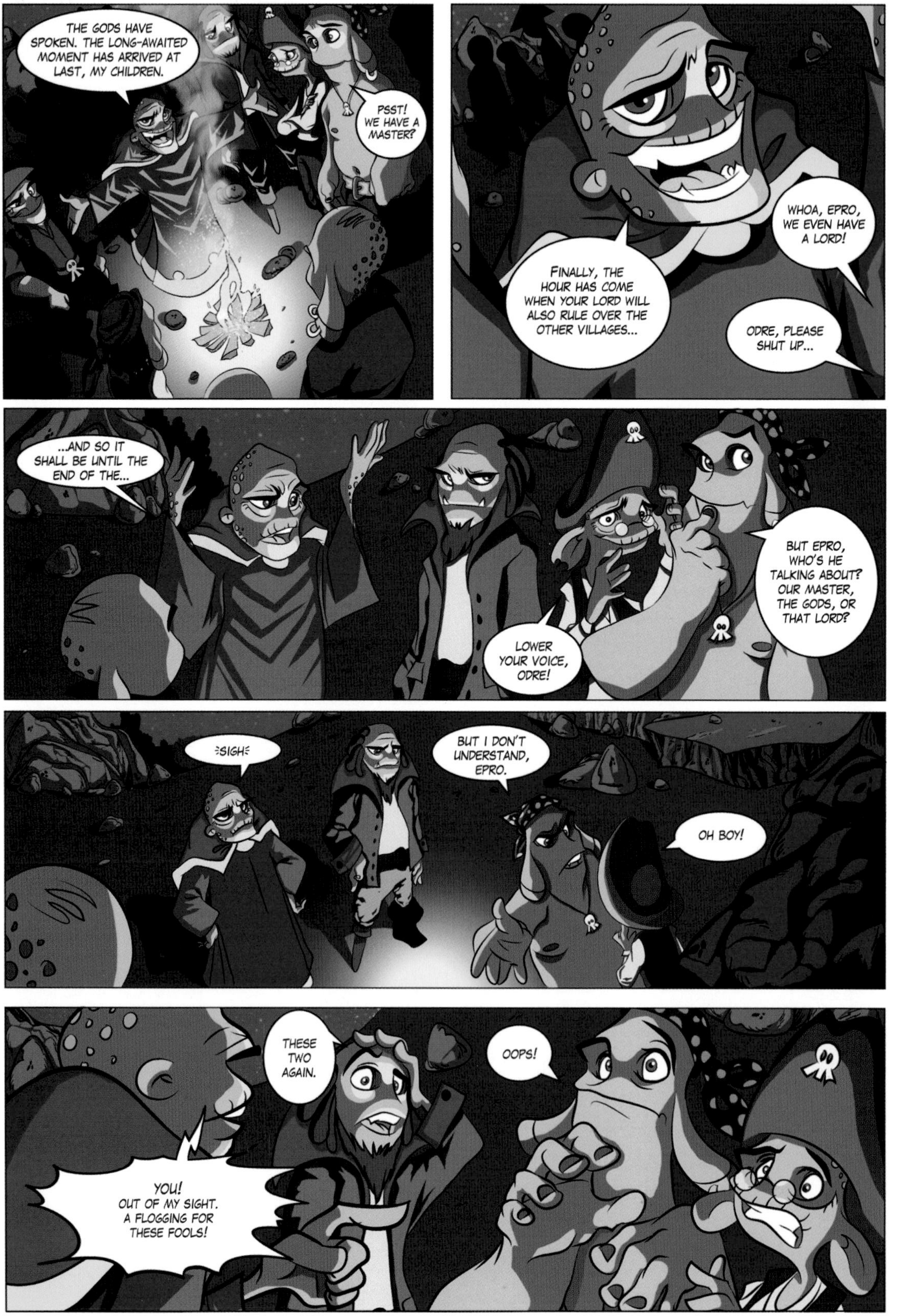
THE GODS HAVE SPOKEN. THE LONG-AWAITED MOMENT HAS ARRIVED AT LAST, MY CHILDREN.
PSST! WE HAVE A MASTER?
FINALLY, THE HOUR HAS COME WHEN YOUR LORD WILL ALSO RULE OVER THE OTHER VILLAGES...
WHOA, EPRO, WE EVEN HAVE A LORD!
ODRE, PLEASE SHUT UP...
...AND SO IT SHALL BE UNTIL THE END OF THE...
BUT EPRO, WHO'S HE TALKING ABOUT? OUR MASTER, THE GODS, OR THAT LORD?
LOWER YOUR VOICE, ODRE!
SIGH
BUT I DON'T UNDERSTAND, EPRO.
OH BOY!
THESE TWO AGAIN.
OOPS!
YOU! OUT OF MY SIGHT. A FLOGGING FOR THESE FOOLS!

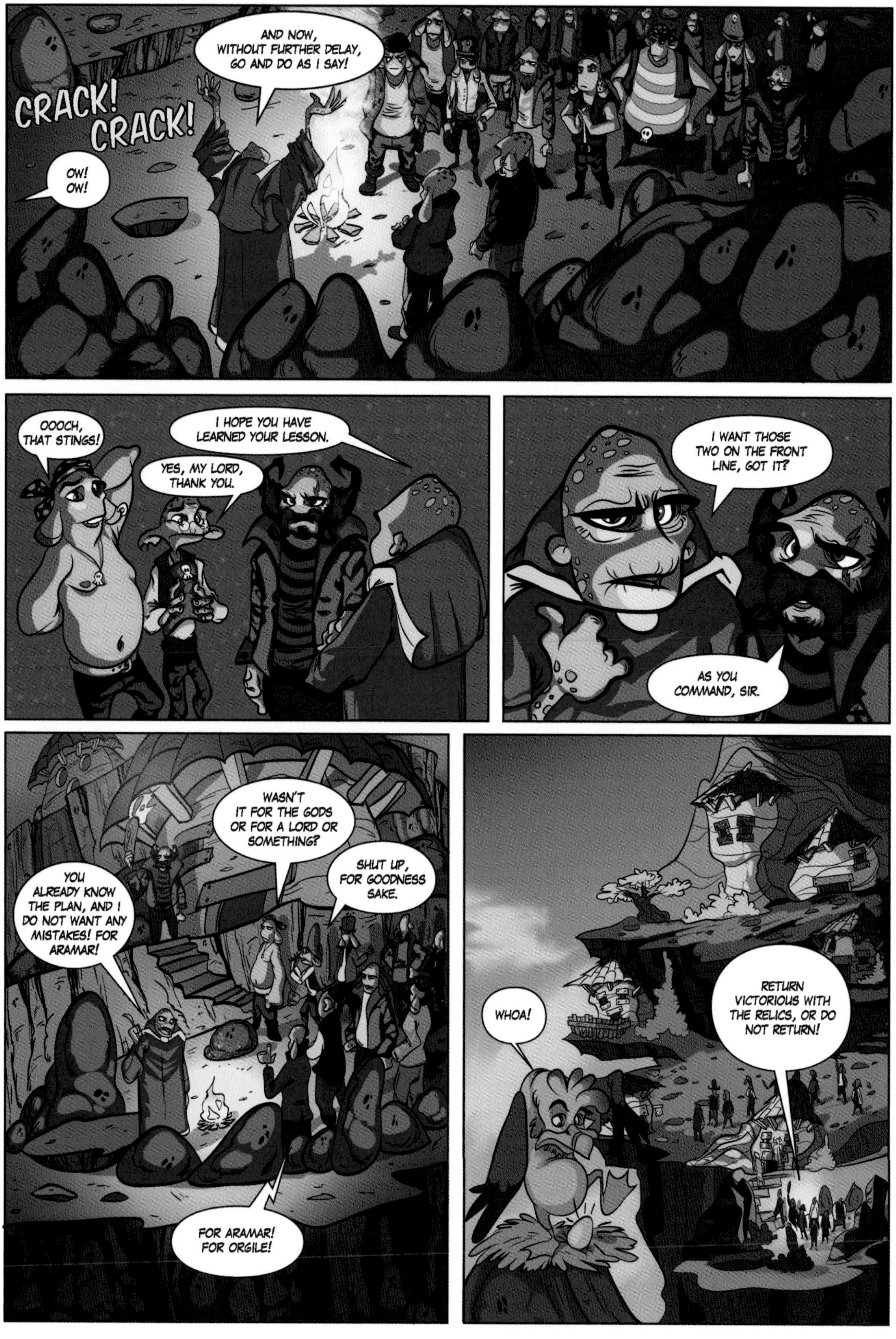
AND NOW, WITHOUT FURTHER DELAY, GO AND DO AS I SAY!
CRACK! CRACK!
OW! OW!
OOOCH, THAT STINGS!
I HOPE YOU HAVE LEARNED YOUR LESSON.
YES, MY LORD, THANK YOU.
I WANT THOSE TWO ON THE FRONT LINE, GOT IT?
AS YOU COMMAND, SIR.
YOU ALREADY KNOW THE PLAN, AND I DO NOT WANT ANY MISTAKES! FOR ARAMAR!
WASN'T IT FOR THE GODS OR FOR A LORD OR SOMETHING?
SHUT UP, FOR GOODNESS SAKE.
FOR ARAMAR! FOR ORGILE!
WHOA!
RETURN VICTORIOUS WITH THE RELICS, OR DO NOT RETURN!

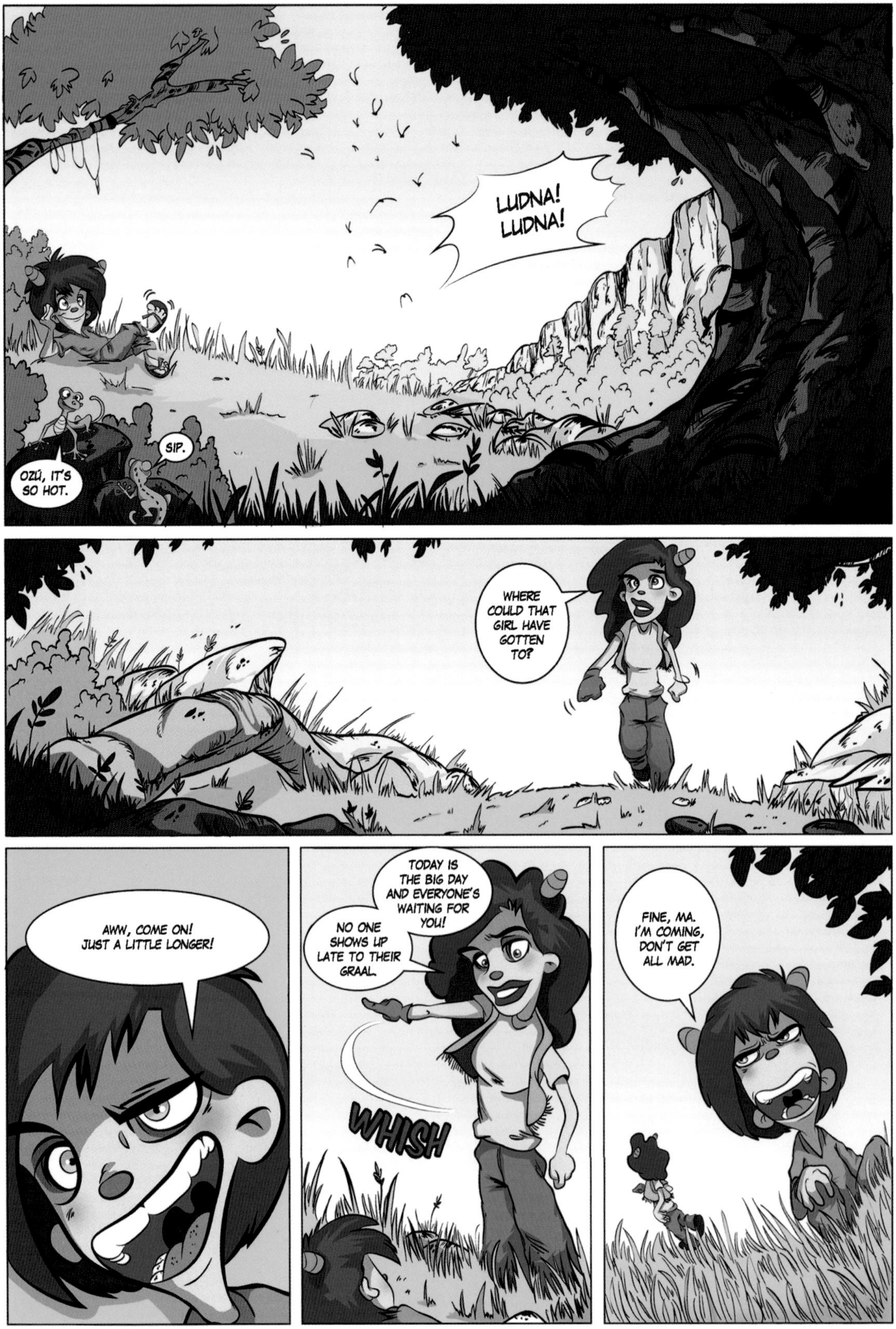
LUDNA! LUDNA!
OZÚ, IT'S SO HOT.
SIP.
WHERE COULD THAT GIRL HAVE GOTTEN TO?
AWW, COME ON! JUST A LITTLE LONGER!
TODAY IS THE BIG DAY AND EVERYONE'S WAITING FOR YOU!
NO ONE SHOWS UP LATE TO THEIR GRAAL.
WHISH
FINE, MA. I'M COMING, DON'T GET ALL MAD.

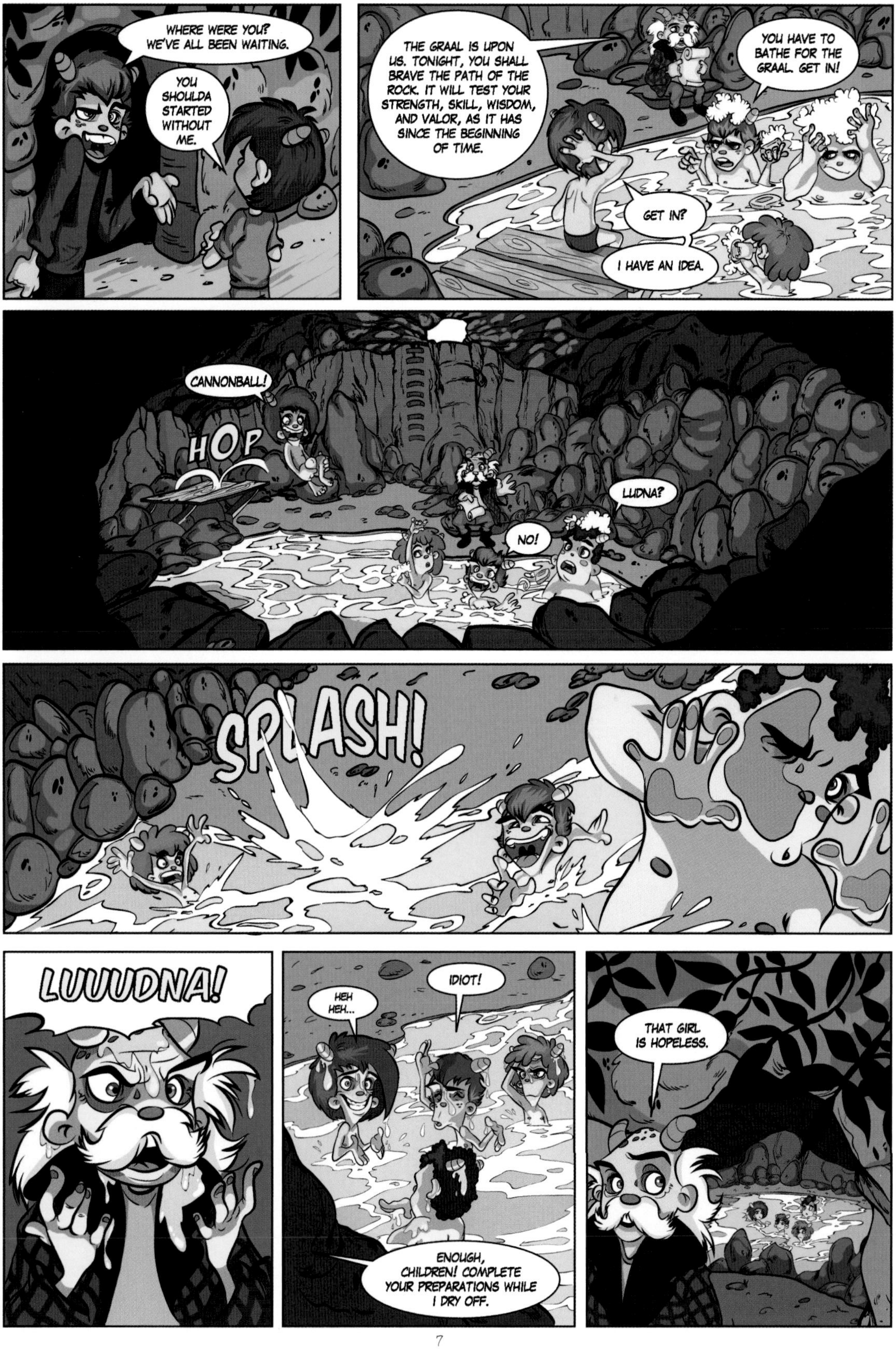

WHERE WERE YOU? WE'VE ALL BEEN WAITING.
YOU SHOULDA STARTED WITHOUT ME.
THE GRAAL IS UPON US. TONIGHT, YOU SHALL BRAVE THE PATH OF THE ROCK. IT WILL TEST YOUR STRENGTH, SKILL, WISDOM, AND VALOR, AS IT HAS SINCE THE BEGINNING OF TIME.
YOU HAVE TO BATHE FOR THE GRAAL. GET IN!
GET IN?
I HAVE AN IDEA.
CANNONBALL!
HOP
LUDNA?
NO!
SPLASH!
LUUUDNA!
HEH HEH...
IDIOT!
ENOUGH, CHILDREN! COMPLETE YOUR PREPARATIONS WHILE I DRY OFF.
THAT GIRL IS HOPELESS.

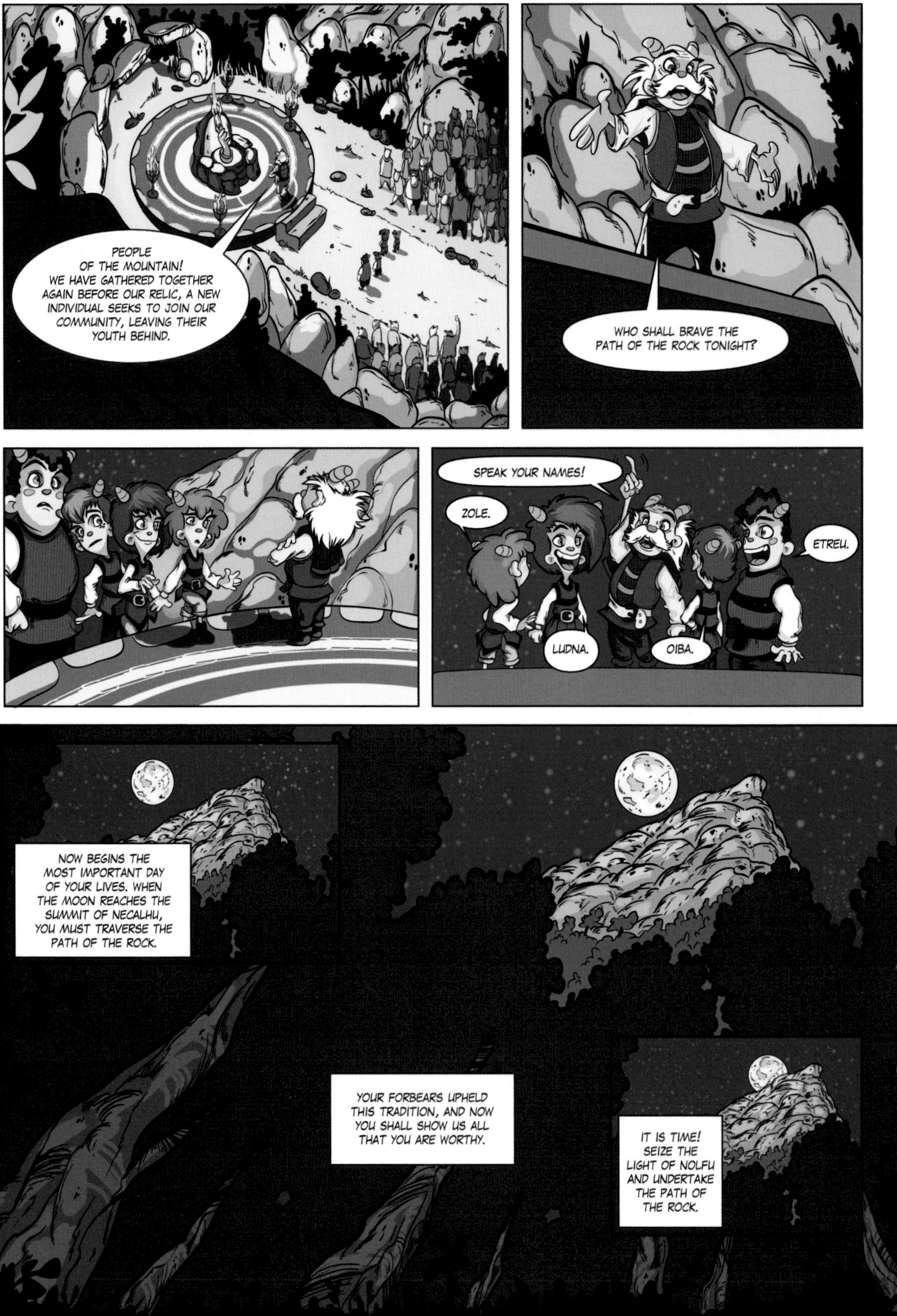
PEOPLE OF THE MOUNTAIN! WE HAVE GATHERED TOGETHER AGAIN BEFORE OUR RELIC, A NEW INDIVIDUAL SEEKS TO JOIN OUR COMMUNITY, LEAVING THEIR YOUTH BEHIND.
WHO SHALL BRAVE THE PATH OF THE ROCK TONIGHT?
SPEAK YOUR NAMES!
ZOLE.
LUDNA.
OIBA.
ETREU.
NOW BEGINS THE MOST IMPORTANT DAY OF YOUR LIVES. WHEN THE MOON REACHES THE SUMMIT OF NECALHU, YOU MUST TRAVERSE THE PATH OF THE ROCK.
YOUR FORBEARS UPHELD THIS TRADITION, AND NOW YOU SHALL SHOW US ALL THAT YOU ARE WORTHY.
IT IS TIME! SEIZE THE LIGHT OF NOLFU AND UNDERTAKE THE PATH OF THE ROCK.

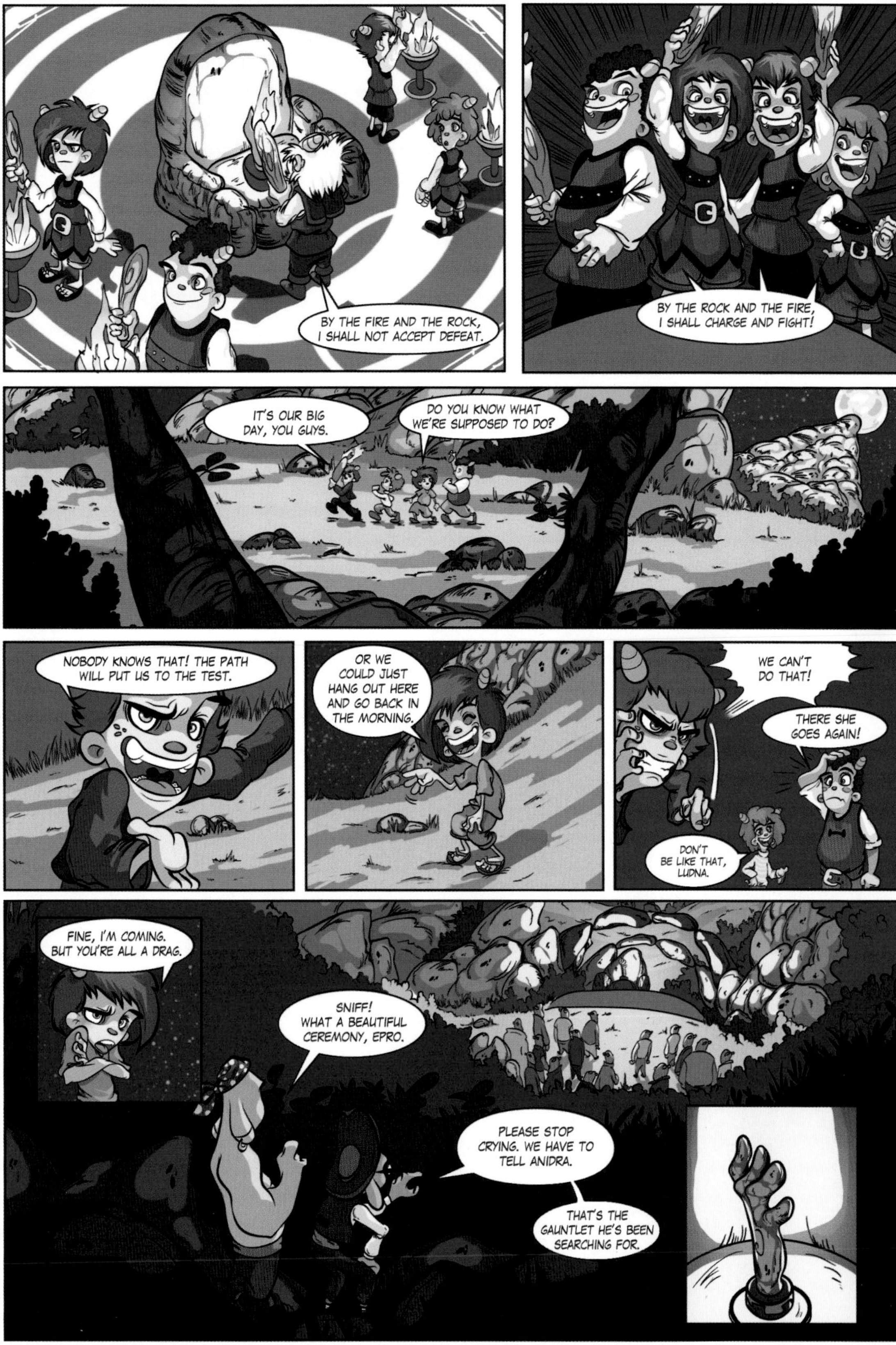
BY THE FIRE AND THE ROCK, I SHALL NOT ACCEPT DEFEAT.
BY THE ROCK AND THE FIRE, I SHALL CHARGE AND FIGHT!
IT'S OUR BIG DAY, YOU GUYS.
DO YOU KNOW WHAT WE'RE SUPPOSED TO DO?
NOBODY KNOWS THAT! THE PATH WILL PUT US TO THE TEST.
OR WE COULD JUST HANG OUT HERE AND GO BACK IN THE MORNING.
WE CAN'T DO THAT!
THERE SHE GOES AGAIN!
DON'T BE LIKE THAT, LUDNA.
FINE, I'M COMING. BUT YOU'RE ALL A DRAG.
SNIFF! WHAT A BEAUTIFUL CEREMONY, EPRO.
PLEASE STOP CRYING. WE HAVE TO TELL ANIDRA.
THAT'S THE GAUNTLET HE'S BEEN SEARCHING FOR.

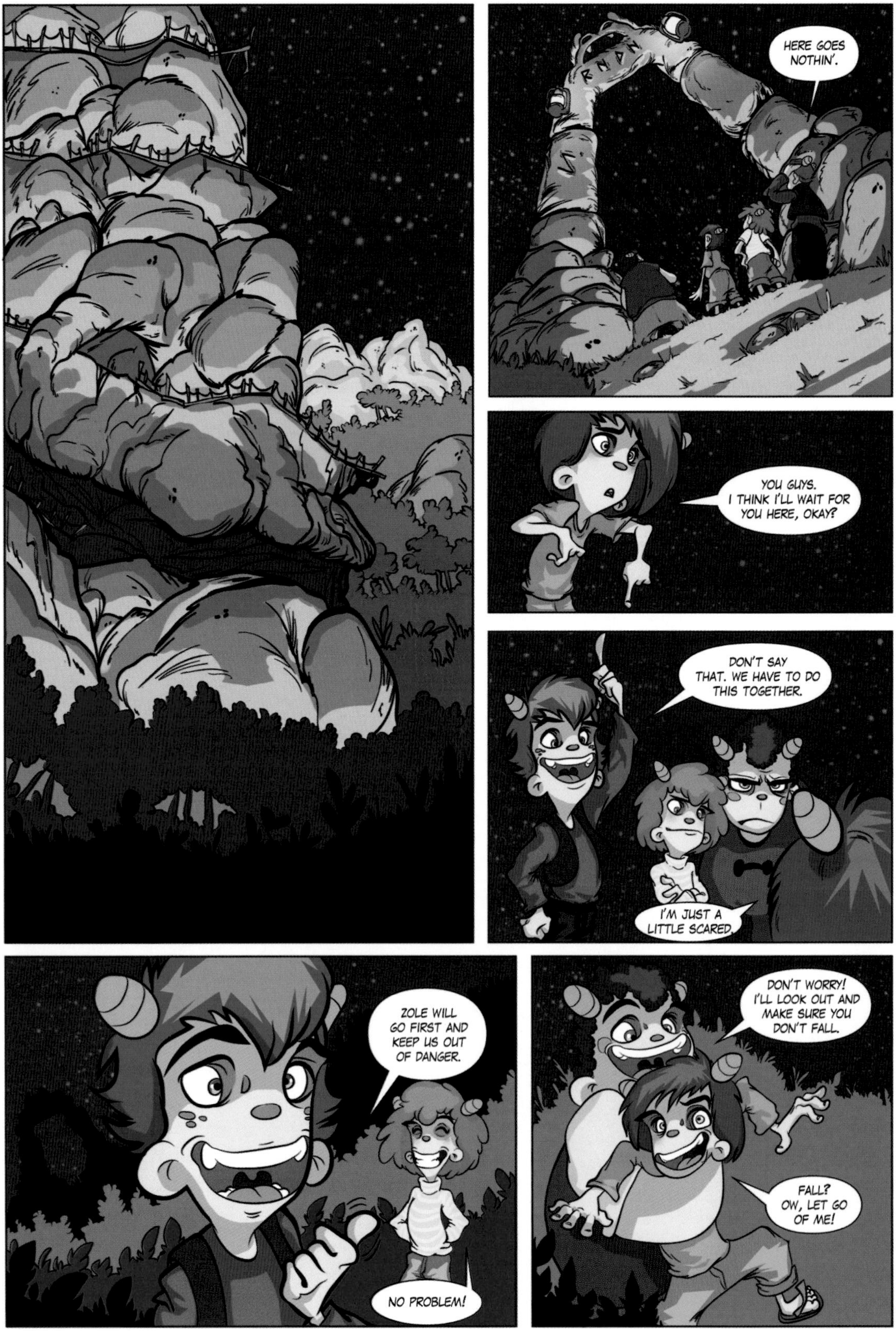

HERE GOES NOTHIN'.
YOU GUYS. I THINK I'LL WAIT FOR YOU HERE, OKAY?
DON'T SAY THAT. WE HAVE TO DO THIS TOGETHER.
I'M JUST A LITTLE SCARED.
ZOLE WILL GO FIRST AND KEEP US OUT OF DANGER.
NO PROBLEM!
DON'T WORRY! I'LL LOOK OUT AND MAKE SURE YOU DON'T FALL.
FALL? OW, LET GO OF ME!

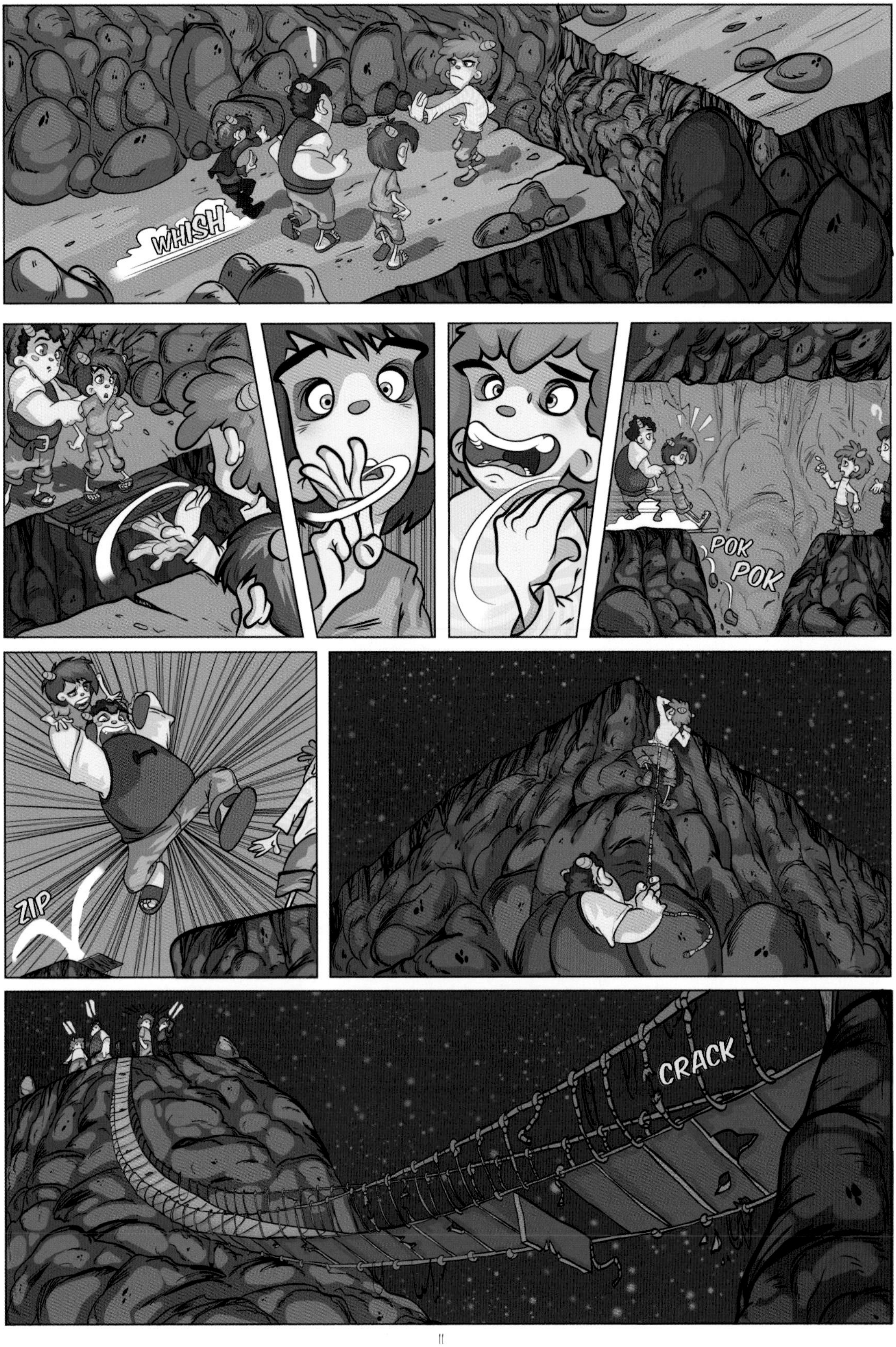
!
WHISH
POK
POK
ZIP
CRACK

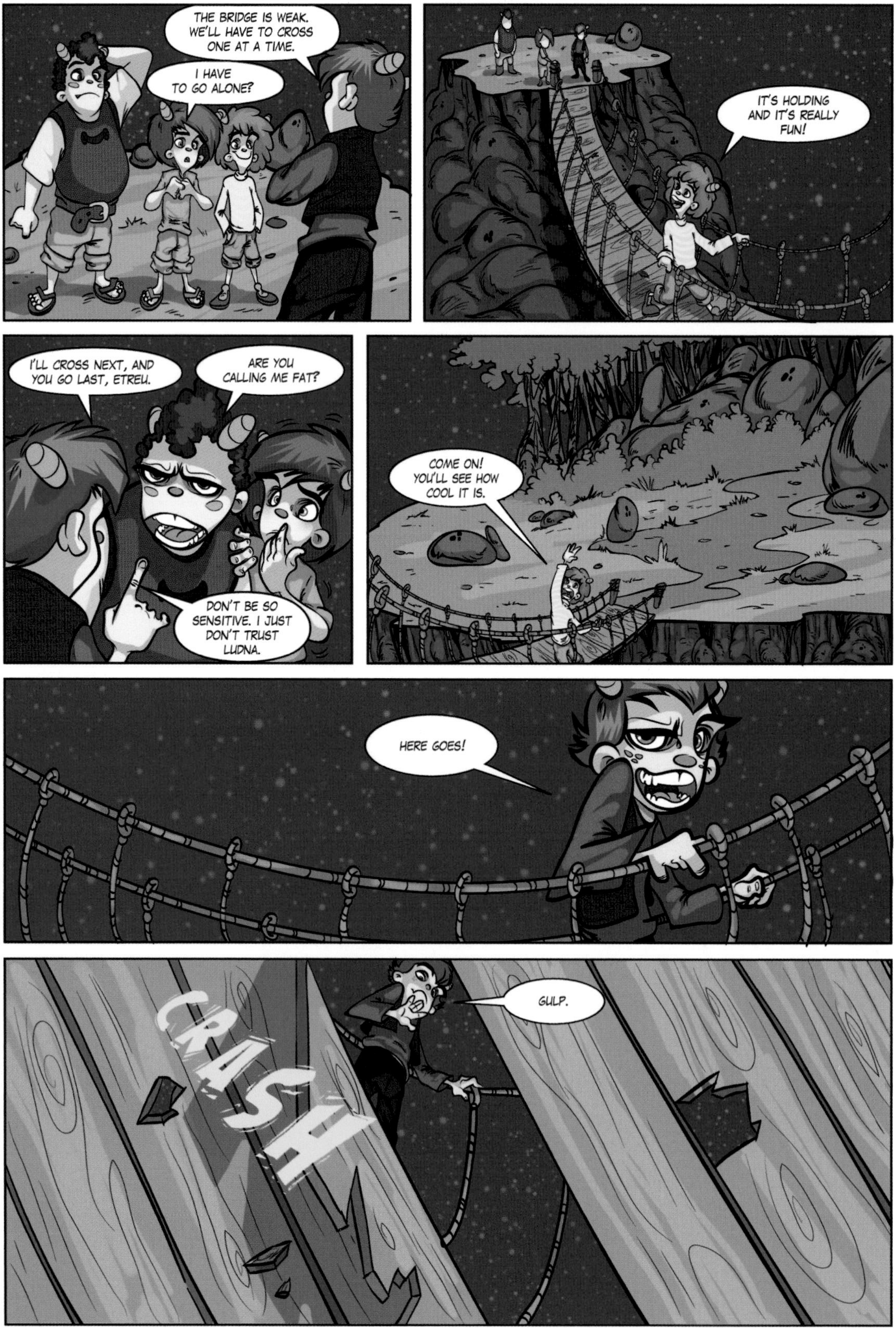
THE BRIDGE IS WEAK. WE'LL HAVE TO CROSS ONE AT A TIME.
I HAVE TO GO ALONE?
IT'S HOLDING AND IT'S REALLY FUN!
I'LL CROSS NEXT, AND YOU GO LAST, ETREU.
ARE YOU CALLING ME FAT?
DON'T BE SO SENSITIVE. I JUST DON'T TRUST LUDNA.
COME ON! YOU'LL SEE HOW COOL IT IS.
HERE GOES!
GULP.
CRASH

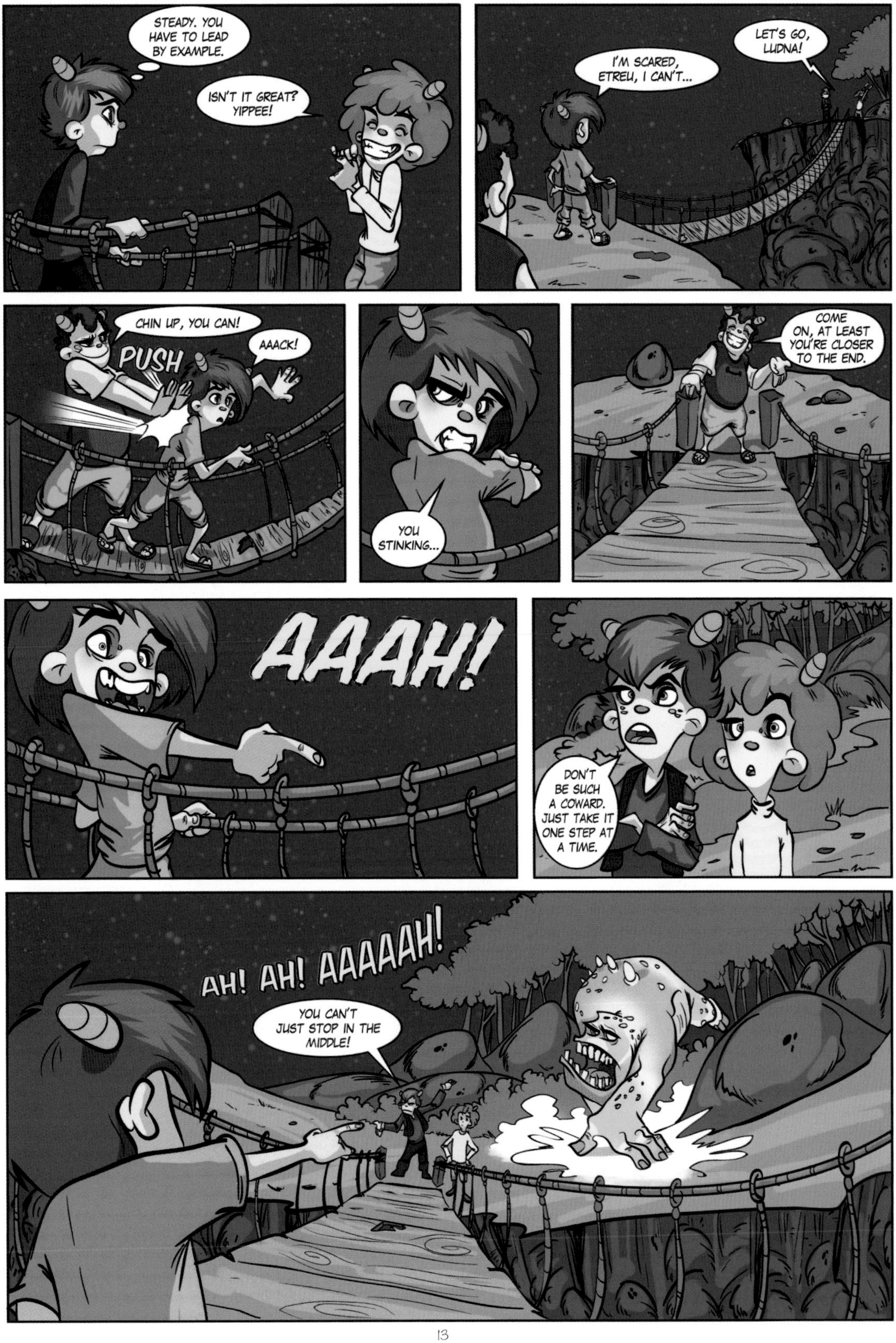
STEADY. YOU HAVE TO LEAD BY EXAMPLE.
ISN'T IT GREAT? YIPPEE!
I'M SCARED, ETREU, I CAN'T...
LET'S GO, LUDNA!
CHIN UP, YOU CAN!
PUSH
AAACK!
YOU STINKING...
COME ON, AT LEAST YOU'RE CLOSER TO THE END.
AAAH!
DON'T BE SUCH A COWARD. JUST TAKE IT ONE STEP AT A TIME.
AH! AH! AAAAAH!
YOU CAN'T JUST STOP IN THE MIDDLE!

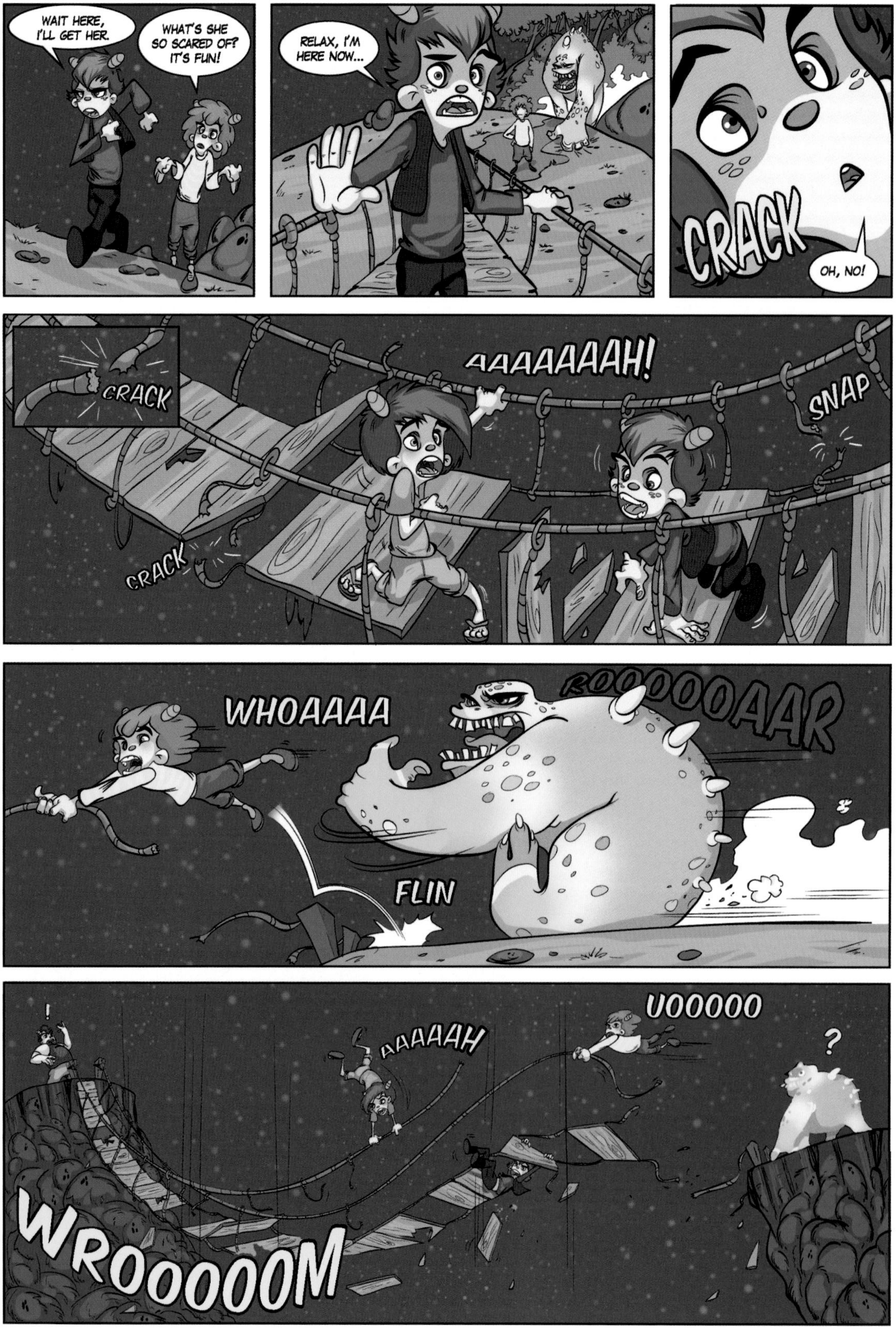
WAIT HERE, I'LL GET HER.
WHAT'S SHE SO SCARED OF? IT'S FUN!
RELAX, I'M HERE NOW...
CRACK
OH, NO!
CRACK
AAAAAAAH!
SNAP
CRACK
WHOAAAA
ROOOOOOAAR
FLIN
UOOOOO
AAAAAH
!
?
WROOOOOM

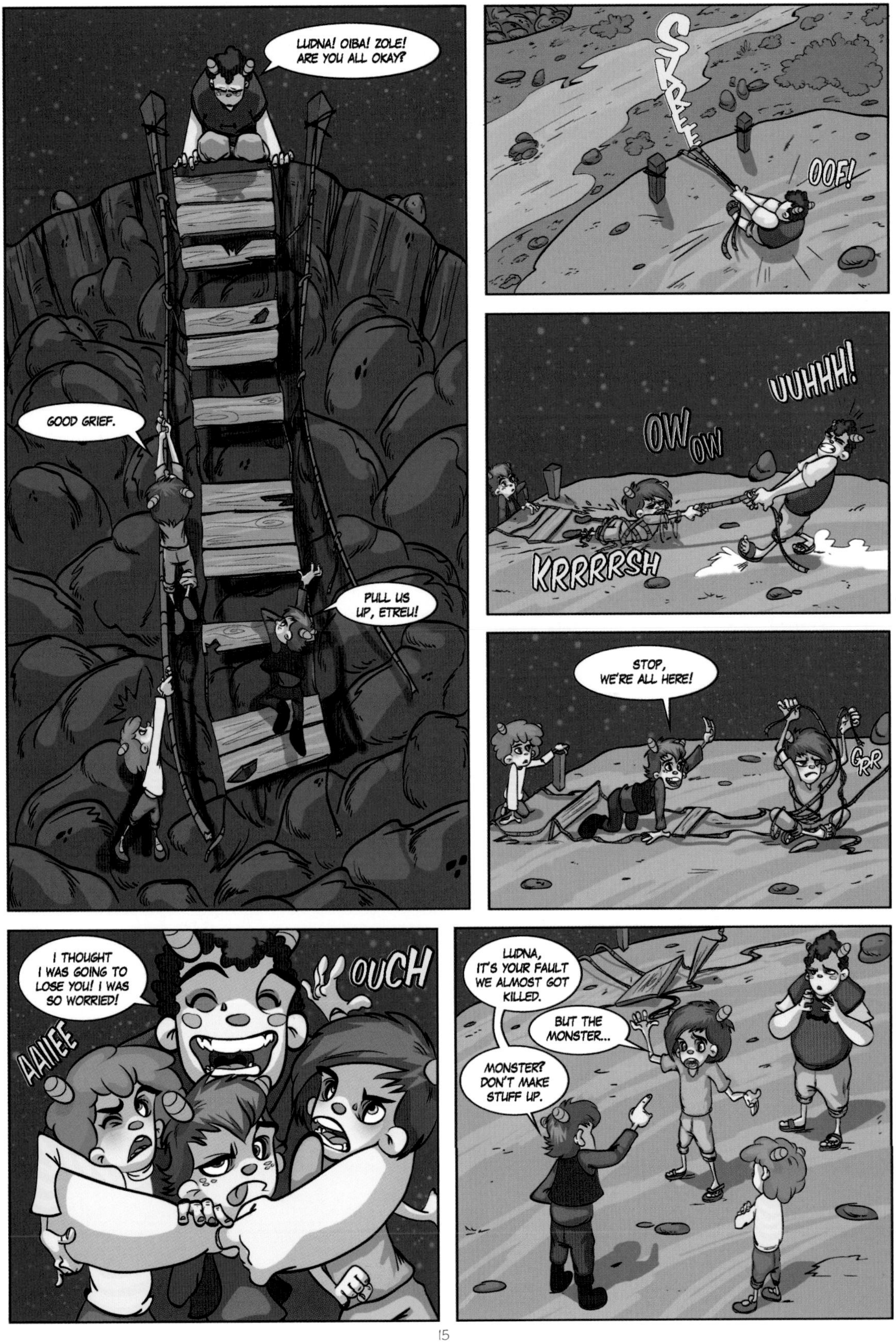
LUDNA! OIBA! ZOLE! ARE YOU ALL OKAY?
GOOD GRIEF.
PULL US UP, ETREU!
SKREE
OOF!
UUHHH!
OW OW
KRRRRSH
STOP, WE'RE ALL HERE!
GRR
I THOUGHT I WAS GOING TO LOSE YOU! I WAS SO WORRIED!
OUCH
AAIIEE
LUDNA, IT'S YOUR FAULT WE ALMOST GOT KILLED.
BUT THE MONSTER...
MONSTER? DON'T MAKE STUFF UP.

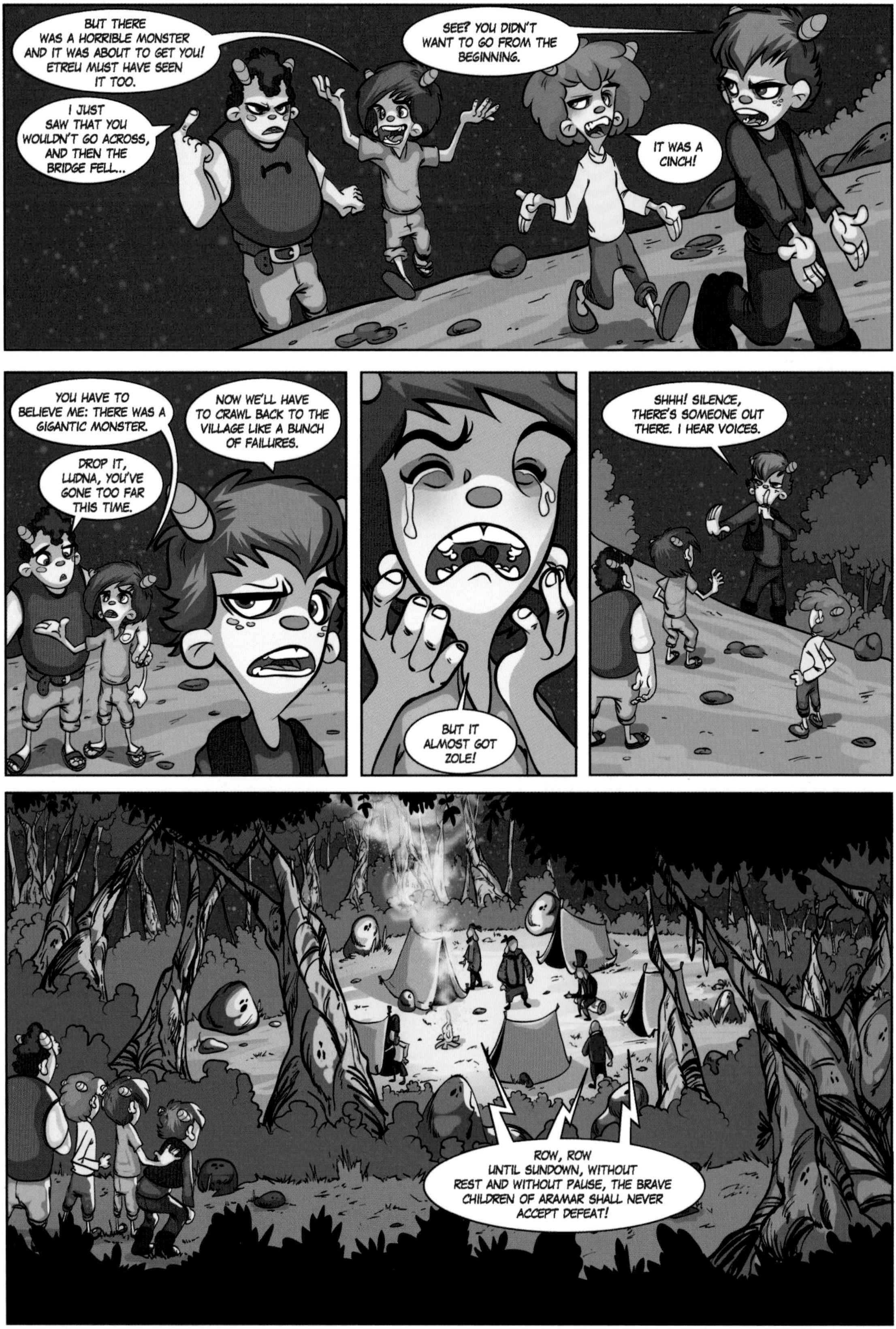
BUT THERE WAS A HORRIBLE MONSTER AND IT WAS ABOUT TO GET YOU! ETREU MUST HAVE SEEN IT TOO.
I JUST SAW THAT YOU WOULDN'T GO ACROSS, AND THEN THE BRIDGE FELL...
SEE? YOU DIDN'T WANT TO GO FROM THE BEGINNING.
IT WAS A CINCH!
YOU HAVE TO BELIEVE ME: THERE WAS A GIGANTIC MONSTER.
DROP IT, LUDNA, YOU'VE GONE TOO FAR THIS TIME.
NOW WE'LL HAVE TO CRAWL BACK TO THE VILLAGE LIKE A BUNCH OF FAILURES.
BUT IT ALMOST GOT ZOLE!
SHHH! SILENCE, THERE'S SOMEONE OUT THERE. I HEAR VOICES.
ROW, ROW UNTIL SUNDOWN, WITHOUT REST AND WITHOUT PAUSE, THE BRAVE CHILDREN OF ARAMAR SHALL NEVER ACCEPT DEFEAT!

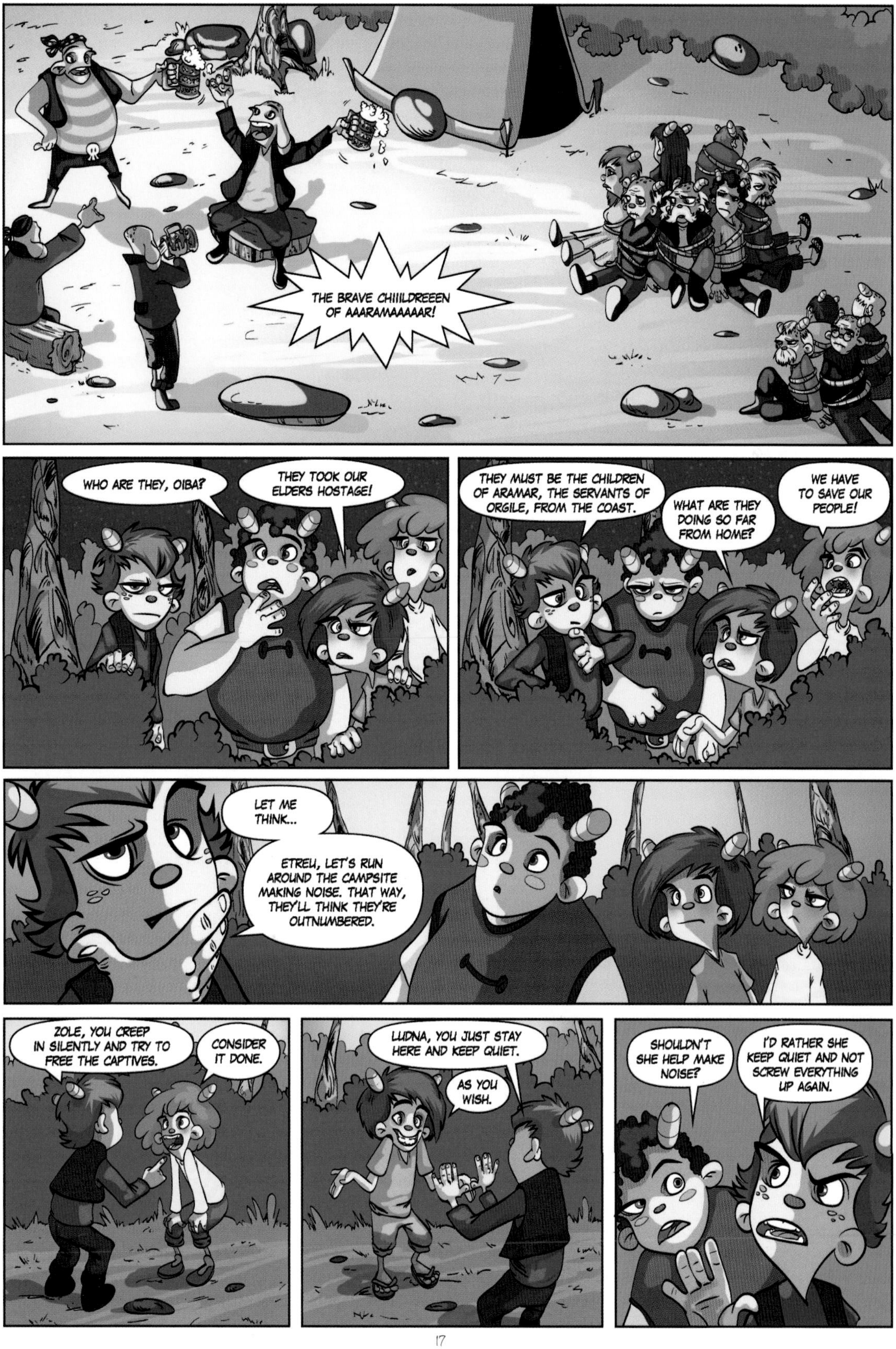
THE BRAVE CHIIILDREEEN OF AAARAMAAAAAR!
WHO ARE THEY, OIBA?
THEY TOOK OUR ELDERS HOSTAGE!
THEY MUST BE THE CHILDREN OF ARAMAR, THE SERVANTS OF ORGILE, FROM THE COAST.
WHAT ARE THEY DOING SO FAR FROM HOME?
WE HAVE TO SAVE OUR PEOPLE!
LET ME THINK...
ETREU, LET'S RUN AROUND THE CAMPSITE MAKING NOISE. THAT WAY, THEY'LL THINK THEY'RE OUTNUMBERED.
ZOLE, YOU CREEP IN SILENTLY AND TRY TO FREE THE CAPTIVES.
CONSIDER IT DONE.
LUDNA, YOU JUST STAY HERE AND KEEP QUIET.
AS YOU WISH.
SHOULDN'T SHE HELP MAKE NOISE?
I'D RATHER SHE KEEP QUIET AND NOT SCREW EVERYTHING UP AGAIN.

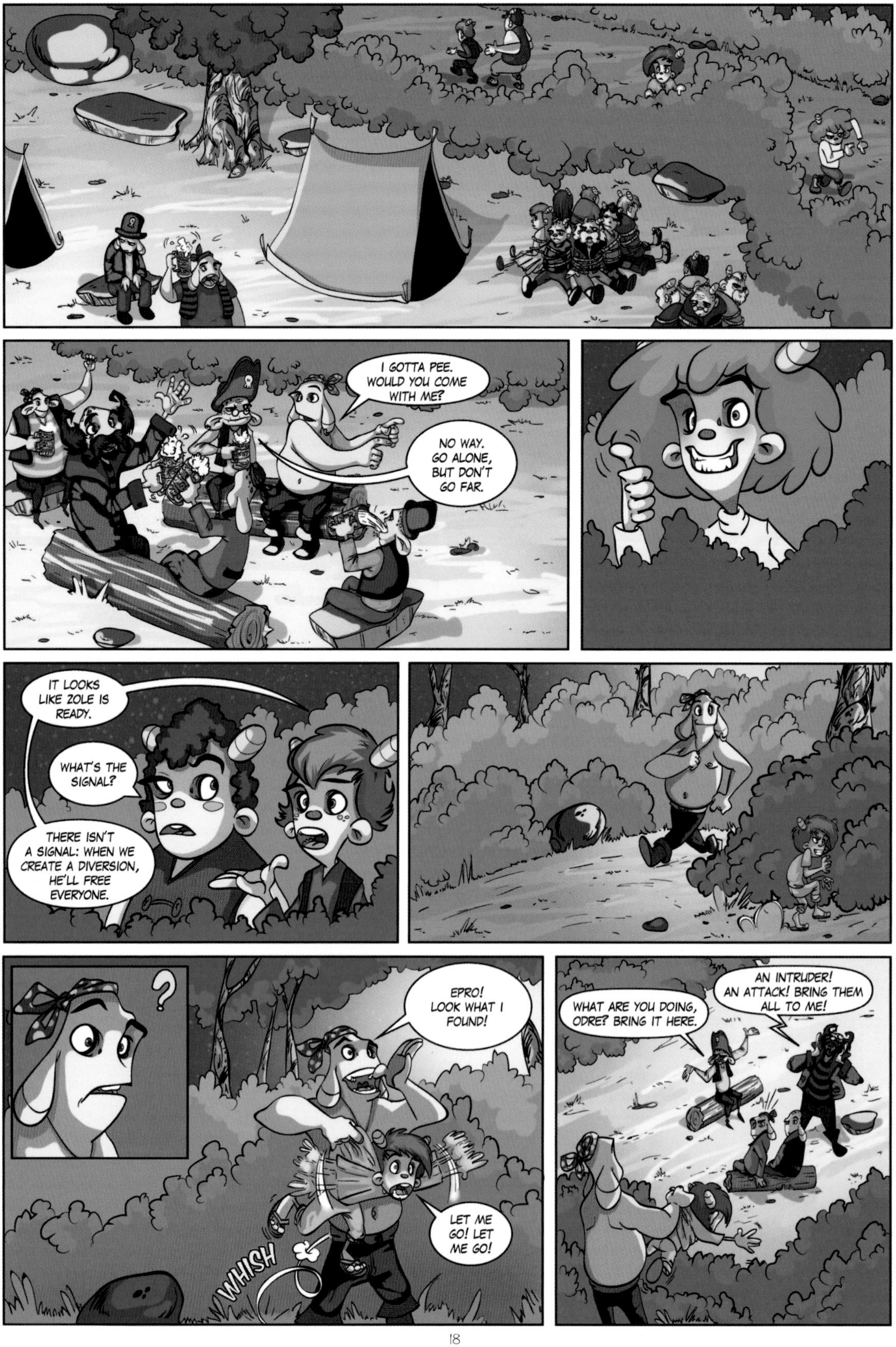
I GOTTA PEE. WOULD YOU COME WITH ME?
NO WAY. GO ALONE, BUT DON'T GO FAR.
IT LOOKS LIKE ZOLE IS READY.
WHAT'S THE SIGNAL?
THERE ISN'T A SIGNAL: WHEN WE CREATE A DIVERSION, HE'LL FREE EVERYONE.
?
EPRO! LOOK WHAT I FOUND!
LET ME GO! LET ME GO!
WHISH
WHAT ARE YOU DOING, ODRE? BRING IT HERE.
AN INTRUDER! AN ATTACK! BRING THEM ALL TO ME!

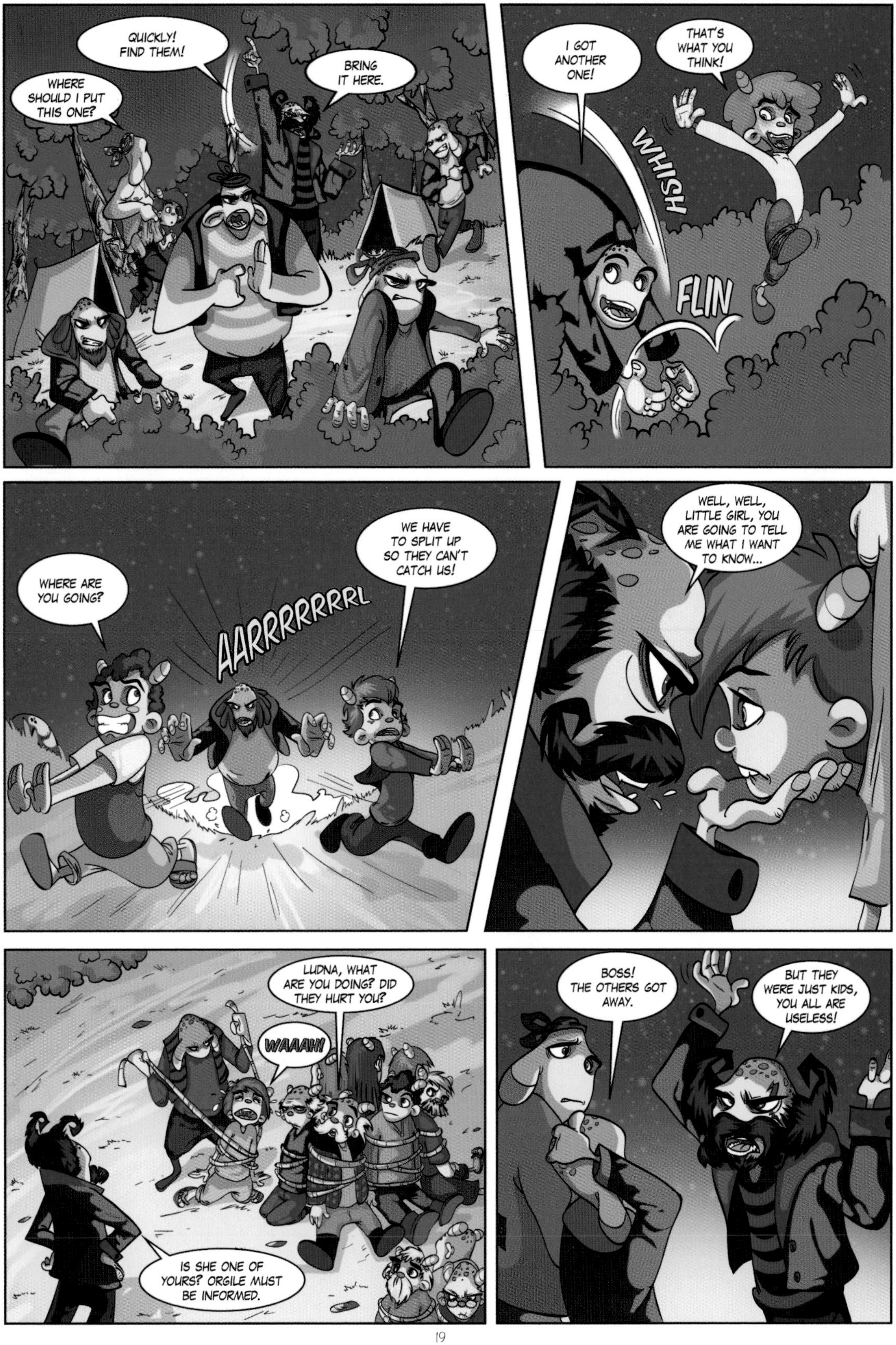
QUICKLY! FIND THEM!
WHERE SHOULD I PUT THIS ONE?
BRING IT HERE.
I GOT ANOTHER ONE!
THAT'S WHAT YOU THINK!
WHISH
FLIN
WHERE ARE YOU GOING?
AARRRRRRRL
WE HAVE TO SPLIT UP SO THEY CAN'T CATCH US!
WELL, WELL, LITTLE GIRL, YOU ARE GOING TO TELL ME WHAT I WANT TO KNOW...
LUDNA, WHAT ARE YOU DOING? DID THEY HURT YOU?
WAAAH!
IS SHE ONE OF YOURS? ORGILE MUST BE INFORMED.
BOSS! THE OTHERS GOT AWAY.
BUT THEY WERE JUST KIDS, YOU ALL ARE USELESS!

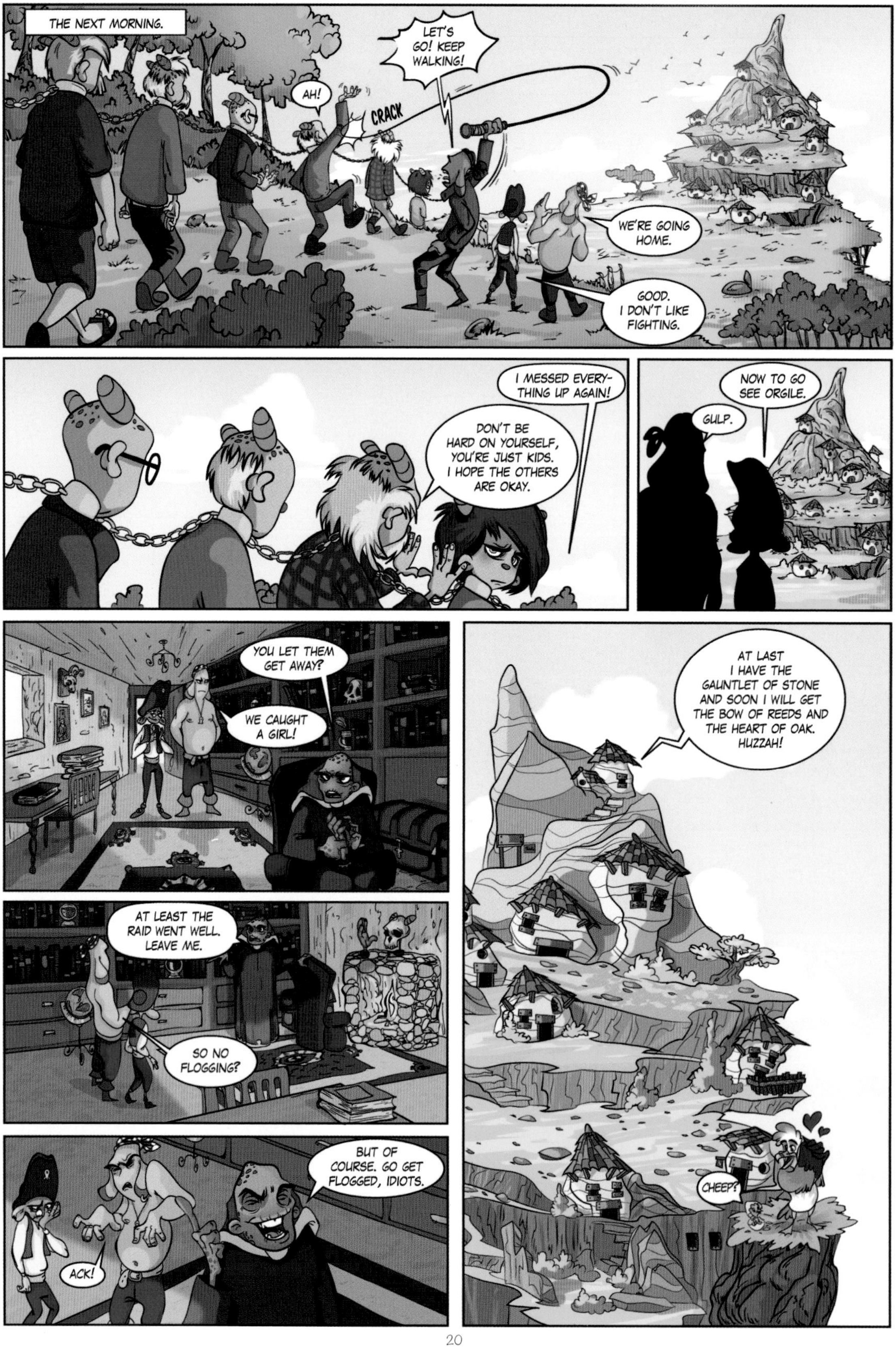
THE NEXT MORNING.
LET'S GO! KEEP WALKING!
AH!
CRACK
WE'RE GOING HOME.
GOOD. I DON'T LIKE FIGHTING.
I MESSED EVERY-THING UP AGAIN!
DON'T BE HARD ON YOURSELF, YOU'RE JUST KIDS. I HOPE THE OTHERS ARE OKAY.
NOW TO GO SEE ORGILE.
GULP.
YOU LET THEM GET AWAY?
WE CAUGHT A GIRL!
AT LEAST THE RAID WENT WELL. LEAVE ME.
SO NO FLOGGING?
BUT OF COURSE. GO GET FLOGGED, IDIOTS.
ACK!
AT LAST I HAVE THE GAUNTLET OF STONE AND SOON I WILL GET THE BOW OF REEDS AND THE HEART OF OAK. HUZZAH!
CHEEP?

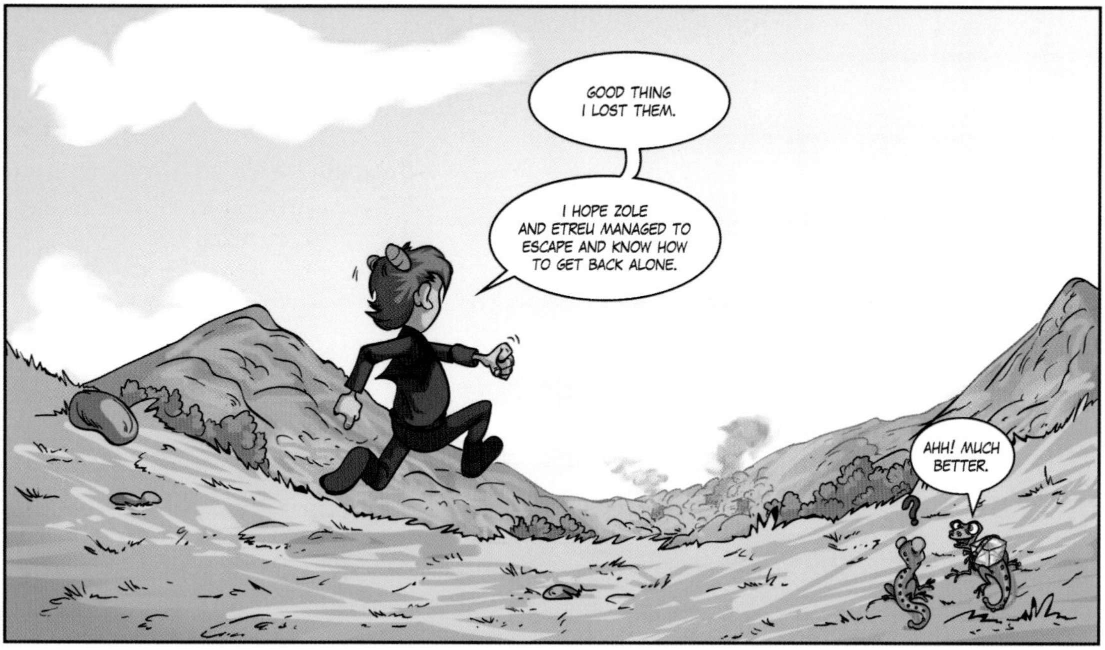
GOOD THING I LOST THEM.
I HOPE ZOLE AND ETREU MANAGED TO ESCAPE AND KNOW HOW TO GET BACK ALONE.
AHH! MUCH BETTER.

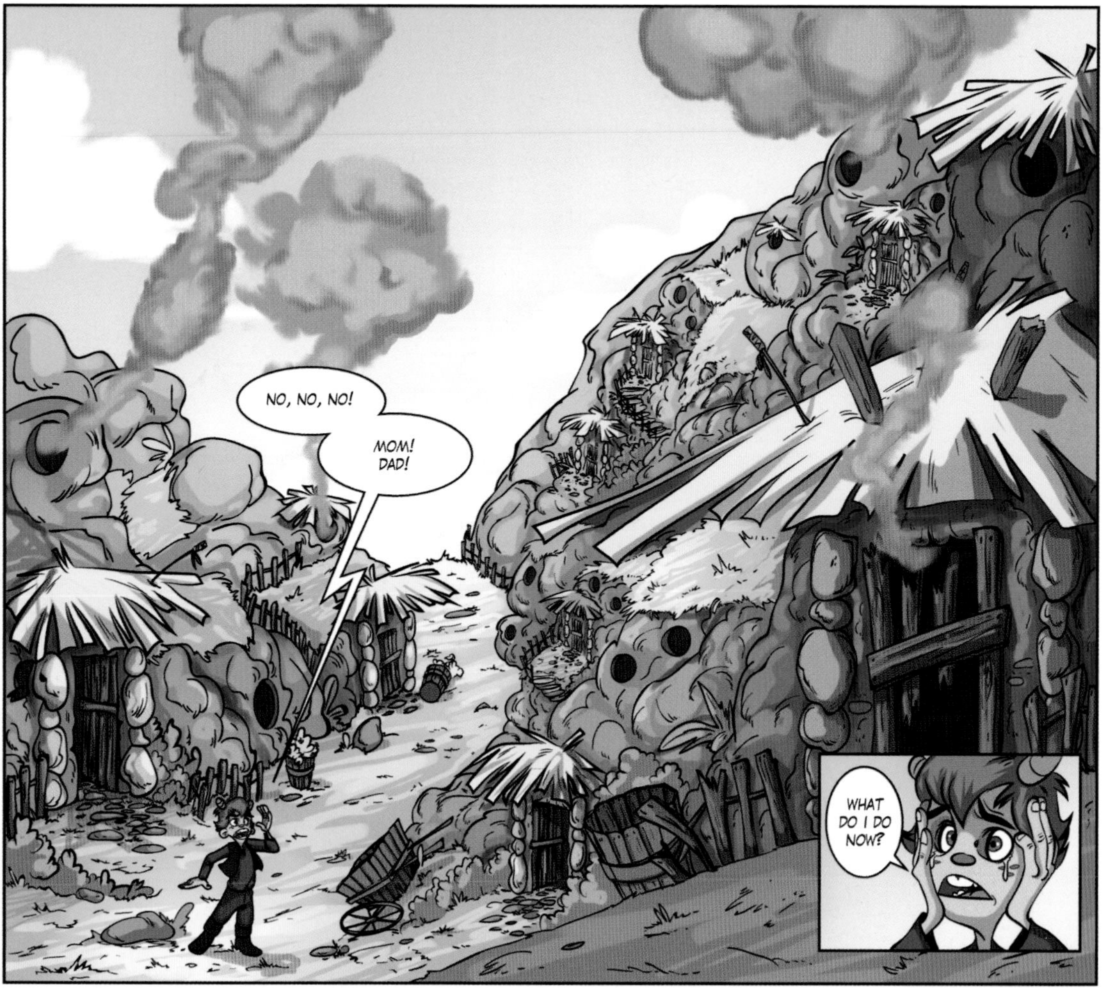
NO, NO, NO!
MOM! DAD!
WHAT DO I DO NOW?

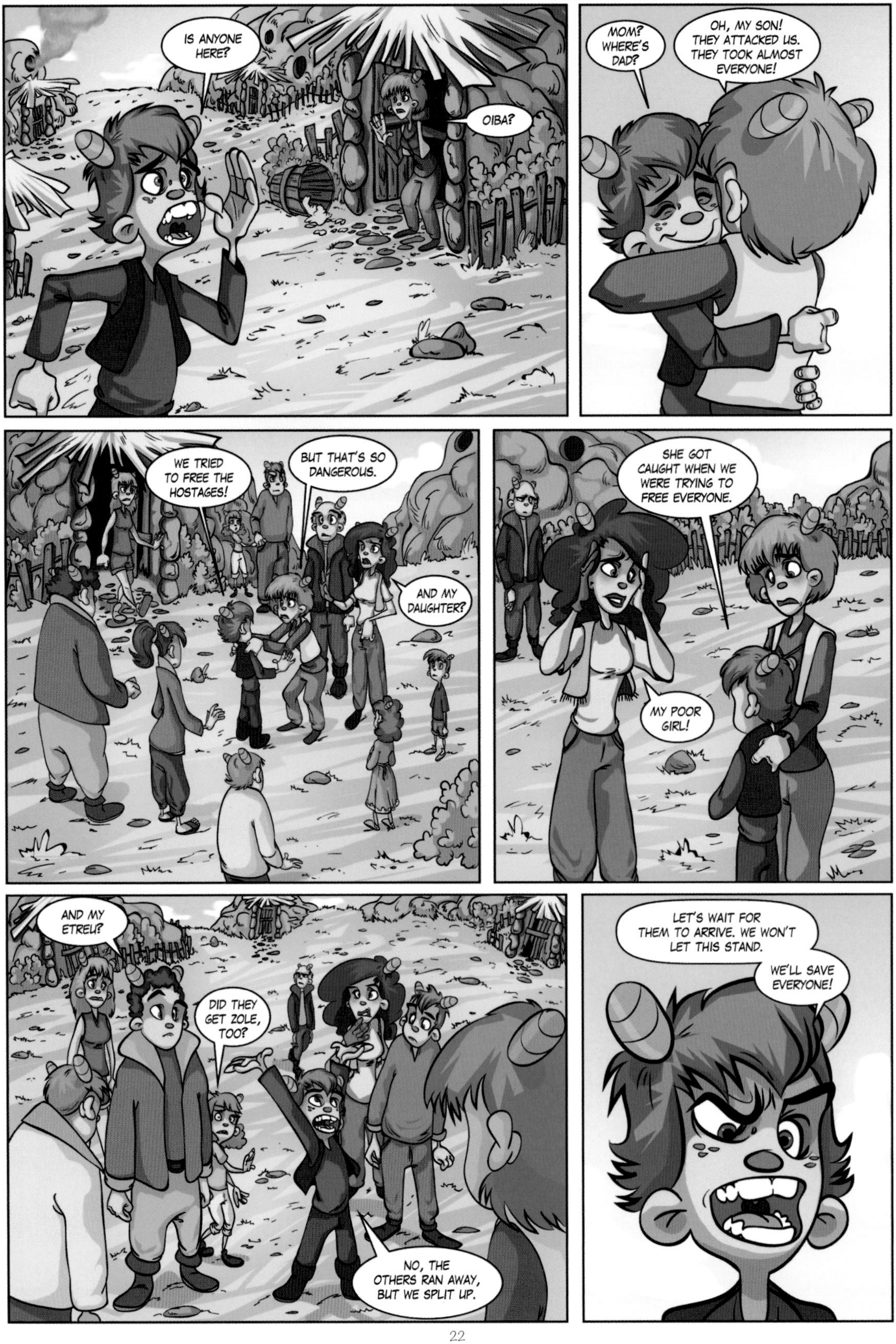
IS ANYONE HERE?
OIBA?
MOM? WHERE'S DAD?
OH, MY SON! THEY ATTACKED US. THEY TOOK ALMOST EVERYONE!
WE TRIED TO FREE THE HOSTAGES!
BUT THAT'S SO DANGEROUS.
AND MY DAUGHTER?
SHE GOT CAUGHT WHEN WE WERE TRYING TO FREE EVERYONE.
MY POOR GIRL!
AND MY ETREU?
DID THEY GET ZOLE, TOO?
NO, THE OTHERS RAN AWAY, BUT WE SPLIT UP.
LET'S WAIT FOR THEM TO ARRIVE. WE WON'T LET THIS STAND.
WE'LL SAVE EVERYONE!

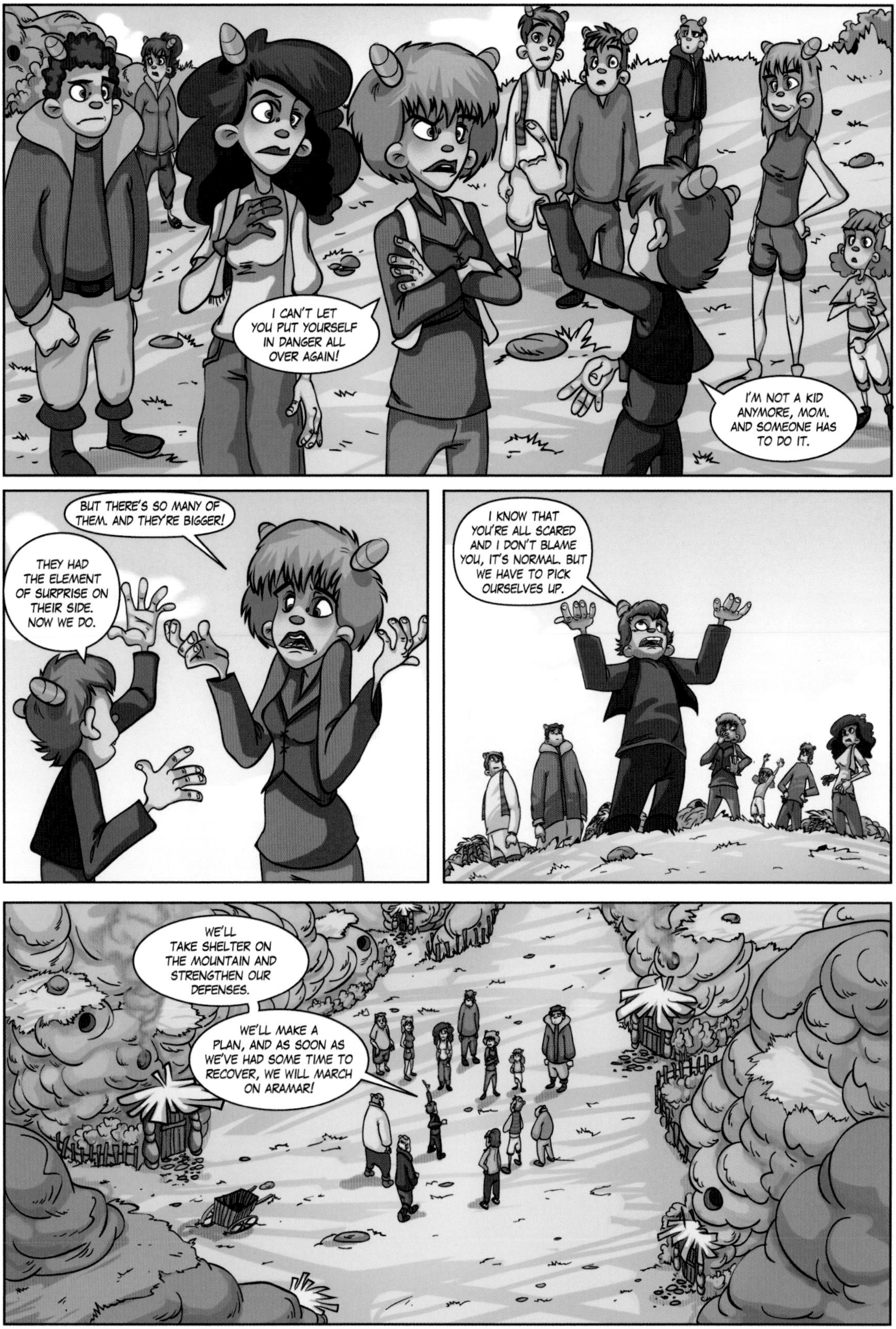
I CAN'T LET YOU PUT YOURSELF IN DANGER ALL OVER AGAIN!
I'M NOT A KID ANYMORE, MOM. AND SOMEONE HAS TO DO IT.
BUT THERE'S SO MANY OF THEM. AND THEY'RE BIGGER!
THEY HAD THE ELEMENT OF SURPRISE ON THEIR SIDE. NOW WE DO.
I KNOW THAT YOU'RE ALL SCARED AND I DON'T BLAME YOU, IT'S NORMAL. BUT WE HAVE TO PICK OURSELVES UP.
WE'LL TAKE SHELTER ON THE MOUNTAIN AND STRENGTHEN OUR DEFENSES.
WE'LL MAKE A PLAN, AND AS SOON AS WE'VE HAD SOME TIME TO RECOVER, WE WILL MARCH ON ARAMAR!

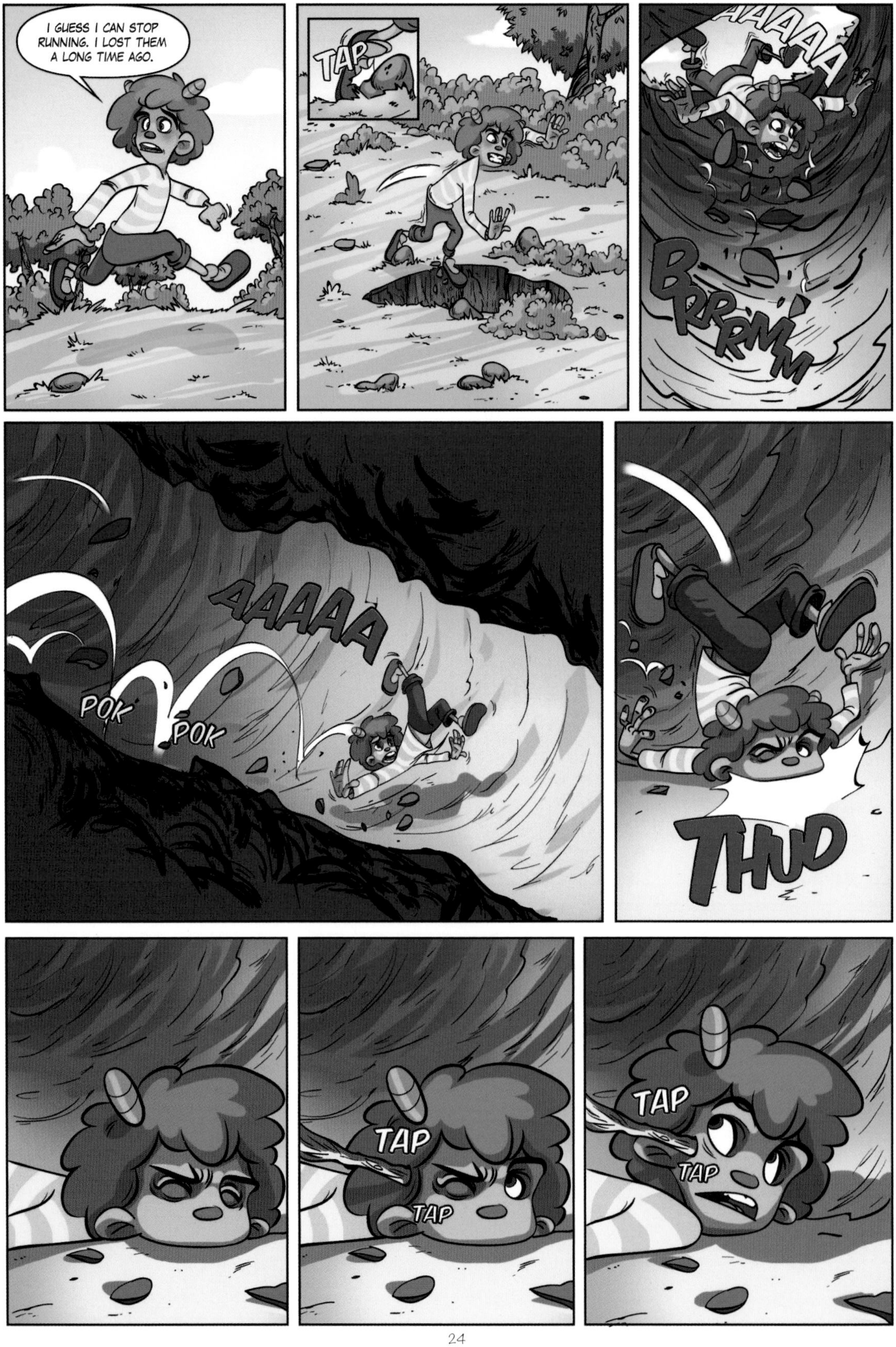

I GUESS I CAN STOP RUNNING. I LOST THEM A LONG TIME AGO.
TAP
AAAAAA
BRRRMM
AAAAA
POK
POK
THUD
TAP
TAP
TAP
TAP

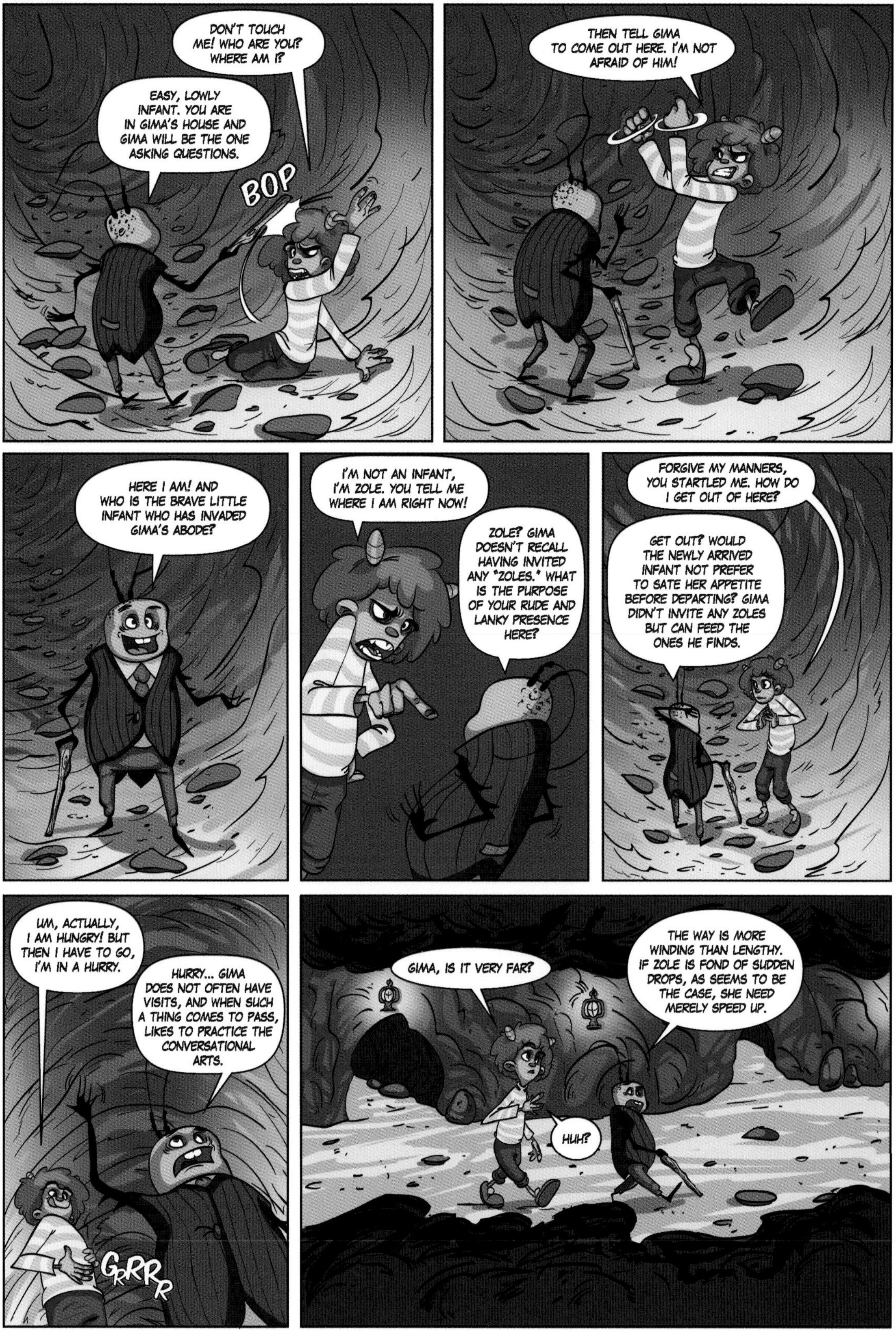
DON'T TOUCH ME! WHO ARE YOU? WHERE AM I?
EASY, LOWLY INFANT. YOU ARE IN GIMA'S HOUSE AND GIMA WILL BE THE ONE ASKING QUESTIONS.
BOP
THEN TELL GIMA TO COME OUT HERE. I'M NOT AFRAID OF HIM!
HERE I AM! AND WHO IS THE BRAVE LITTLE INFANT WHO HAS INVADED GIMA'S ABODE?
I'M NOT AN INFANT, I'M ZOLE. YOU TELL ME WHERE I AM RIGHT NOW!
ZOLE? GIMA DOESN'T RECALL HAVING INVITED ANY "ZOLES." WHAT IS THE PURPOSE OF YOUR RUDE AND LANKY PRESENCE HERE?
FORGIVE MY MANNERS, YOU STARTLED ME. HOW DO I GET OUT OF HERE?
GET OUT? WOULD THE NEWLY ARRIVED INFANT NOT PREFER TO SATE HER APPETITE BEFORE DEPARTING? GIMA DIDN'T INVITE ANY ZOLES BUT CAN FEED THE ONES HE FINDS.
UM, ACTUALLY, I AM HUNGRY! BUT THEN I HAVE TO GO, I'M IN A HURRY.
HURRY... GIMA DOES NOT OFTEN HAVE VISITS, AND WHEN SUCH A THING COMES TO PASS, LIKES TO PRACTICE THE CONVERSATIONAL ARTS.
GRRRR
GIMA, IS IT VERY FAR?
THE WAY IS MORE WINDING THAN LENGTHY. IF ZOLE IS FOND OF SUDDEN DROPS, AS SEEMS TO BE THE CASE, SHE NEED MERELY SPEED UP.
HUH?

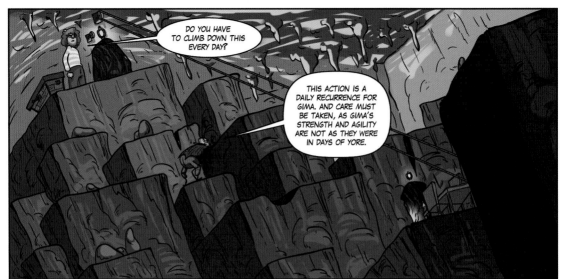

DO YOU HAVE TO CLIMB DOWN THIS EVERY DAY?

THIS ACTION IS A DAILY RECURRENCE FOR GIMA. AND CARE MUST BE TAKEN, AS GIMA'S STRENGTH AND AGILITY ARE NOT AS THEY WERE IN DAYS OF YORE.

YIPPEEEE

IMPOLITE INFANT! ABSTAIN FROM TOUCHING GIMA'S BELONGINGS!

DON'T BE MAD. YOU'LL LIKE THIS, AND YOU WON'T HAVE TO WORK SO HARD TO GET DOWN!

PLUS, YOU CAN GO BACK UP JUST BY PULLING ON THIS CORD.

OH! GIMA PERCEIVES THE UTILITY AND IS VERY GRATEFUL FOR THE ZOLE'S ASSISTANCE.

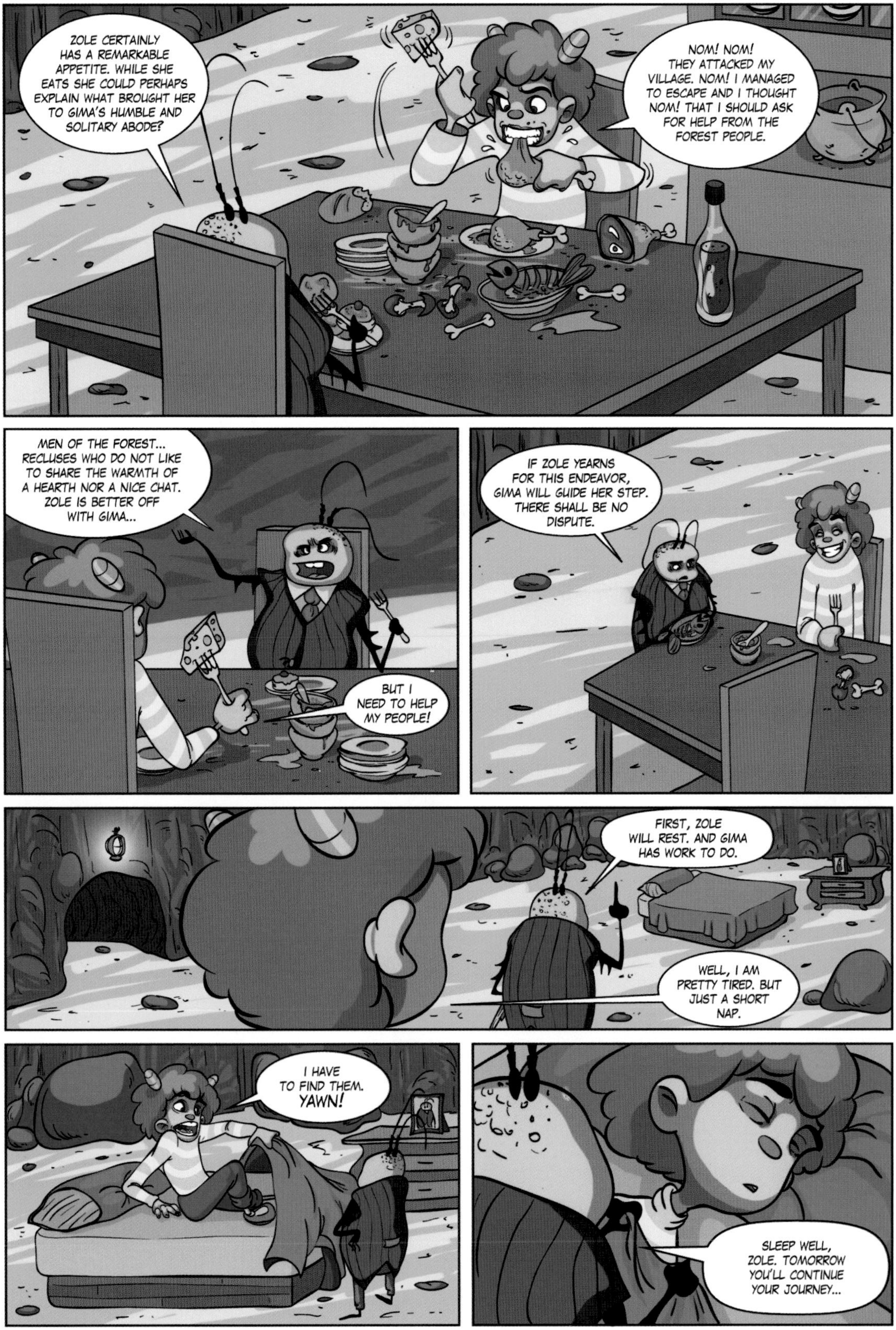
ZOLE CERTAINLY HAS A REMARKABLE APPETITE. WHILE SHE EATS SHE COULD PERHAPS EXPLAIN WHAT BROUGHT HER TO GIMA'S HUMBLE AND SOLITARY ABODE?
NOM! NOM! THEY ATTACKED MY VILLAGE. NOM! I MANAGED TO ESCAPE AND I THOUGHT NOM! THAT I SHOULD ASK FOR HELP FROM THE FOREST PEOPLE.
MEN OF THE FOREST... RECLUSES WHO DO NOT LIKE TO SHARE THE WARMTH OF A HEARTH NOR A NICE CHAT. ZOLE IS BETTER OFF WITH GIMA...
BUT I NEED TO HELP MY PEOPLE!
IF ZOLE YEARNS FOR THIS ENDEAVOR, GIMA WILL GUIDE HER STEP. THERE SHALL BE NO DISPUTE.
FIRST, ZOLE WILL REST. AND GIMA HAS WORK TO DO.
WELL, I AM PRETTY TIRED. BUT JUST A SHORT NAP.
I HAVE TO FIND THEM. YAWN!
SLEEP WELL, ZOLE. TOMORROW YOU'LL CONTINUE YOUR JOURNEY...

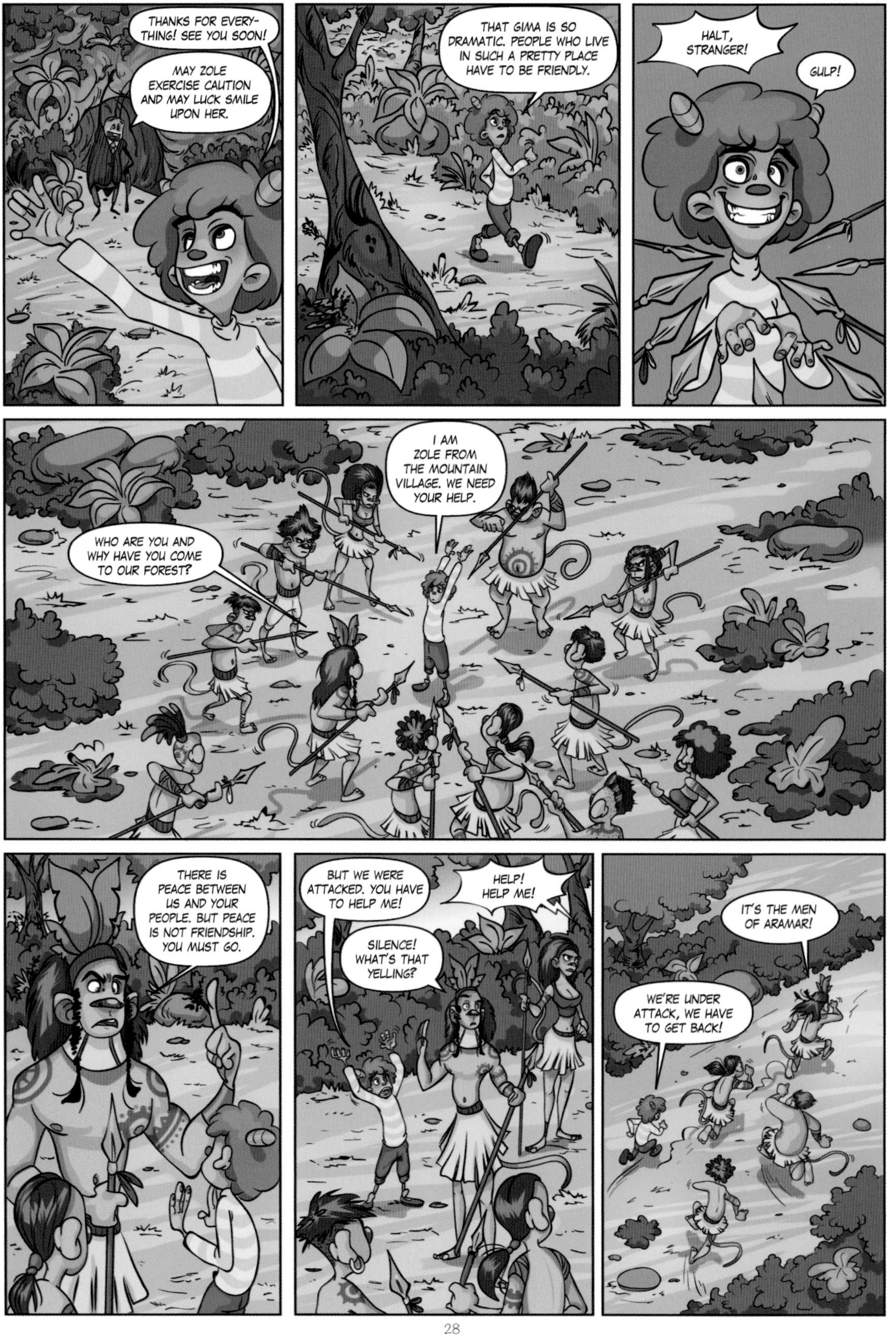
THANKS FOR EVERY-THING! SEE YOU SOON!
MAY ZOLE EXERCISE CAUTION AND MAY LUCK SMILE UPON HER.
THAT GIMA IS SO DRAMATIC. PEOPLE WHO LIVE IN SUCH A PRETTY PLACE HAVE TO BE FRIENDLY.
HALT, STRANGER!
GULP!
WHO ARE YOU AND WHY HAVE YOU COME TO OUR FOREST?
I AM ZOLE FROM THE MOUNTAIN VILLAGE. WE NEED YOUR HELP.
THERE IS PEACE BETWEEN US AND YOUR PEOPLE. BUT PEACE IS NOT FRIENDSHIP. YOU MUST GO.
BUT WE WERE ATTACKED. YOU HAVE TO HELP ME!
HELP! HELP ME!
SILENCE! WHAT'S THAT YELLING?
IT'S THE MEN OF ARAMAR!
WE'RE UNDER ATTACK, WE HAVE TO GET BACK!

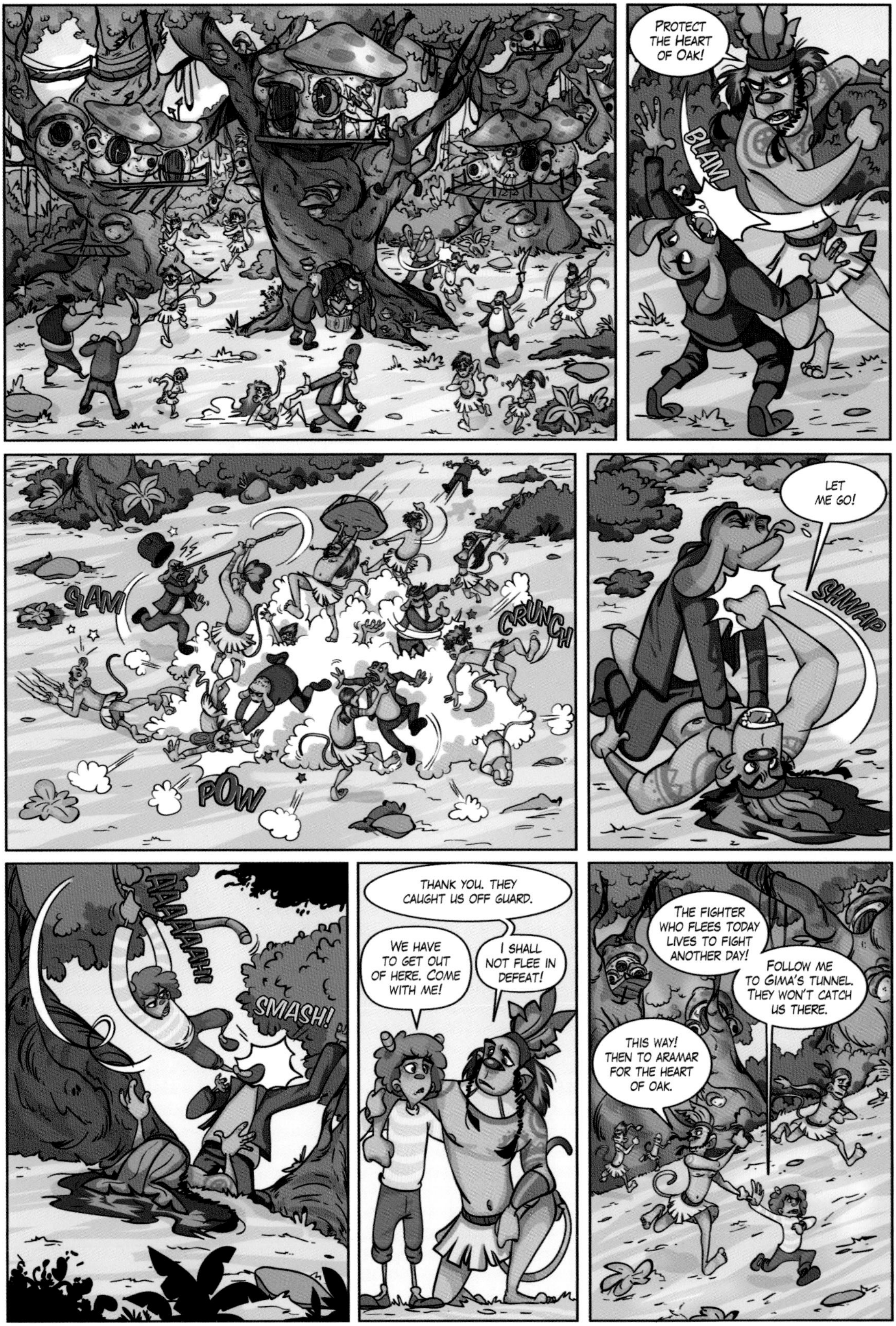
PROTECT THE HEART OF OAK!
BLAM
SLAM
CRUNCH
POW
LET ME GO!
SHWAP
AAAAAAAAH!
SMASH!
THANK YOU. THEY CAUGHT US OFF GUARD.
WE HAVE TO GET OUT OF HERE. COME WITH ME!
I SHALL NOT FLEE IN DEFEAT!
THE FIGHTER WHO FLEES TODAY LIVES TO FIGHT ANOTHER DAY!
FOLLOW ME TO GIMA'S TUNNEL. THEY WON'T CATCH US THERE.
THIS WAY! THEN TO ARAMAR FOR THE HEART OF OAK.

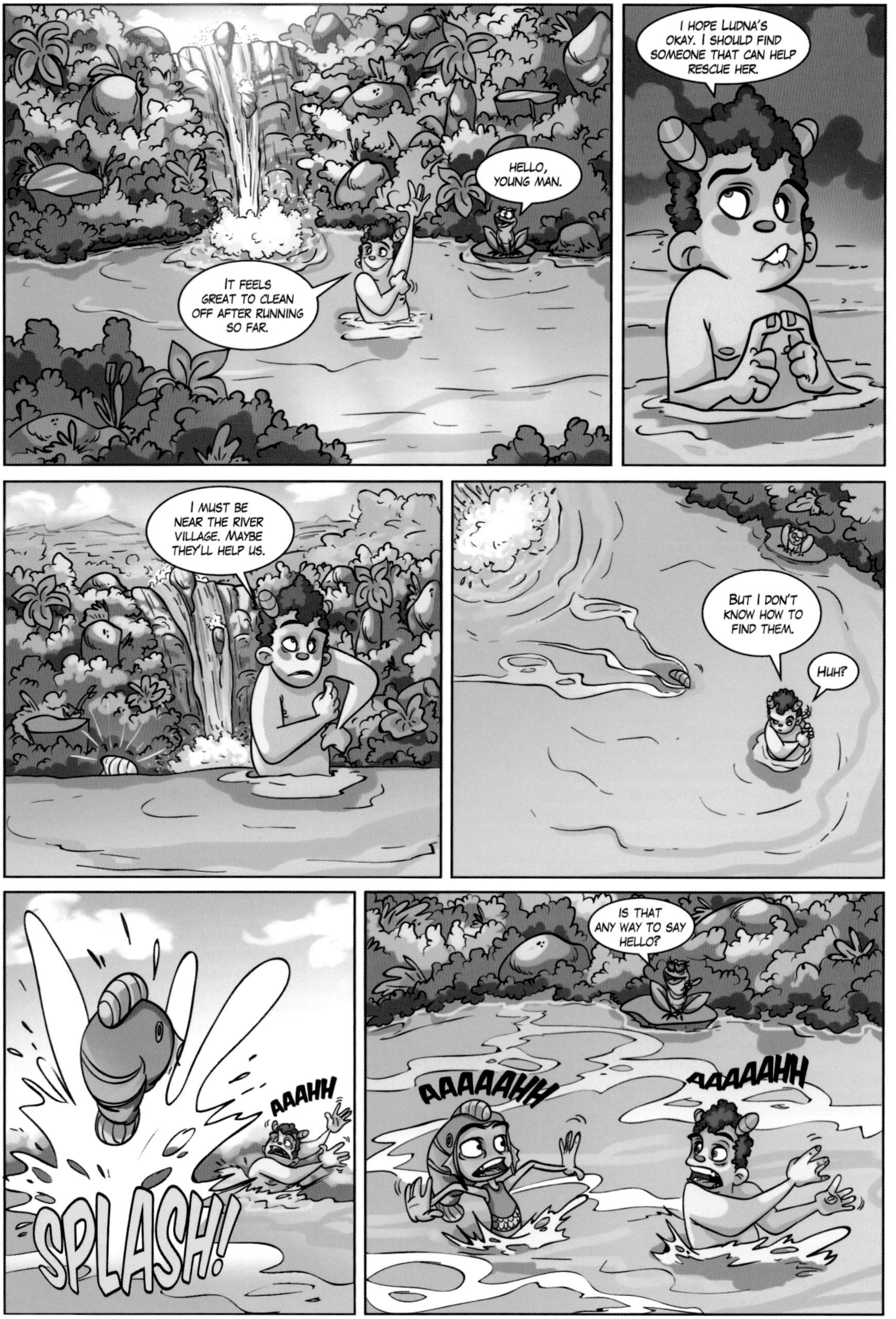
Hello, young man.
It feels great to clean off after running so far.
I hope Ludna's okay. I should find someone that can help rescue her.
I must be near the river village. Maybe they'll help us.
But I don't know how to find them.
Huh?
AAAHH
SPLASH!
Is that any way to say hello?
AAAAAHH
AAAAAHH

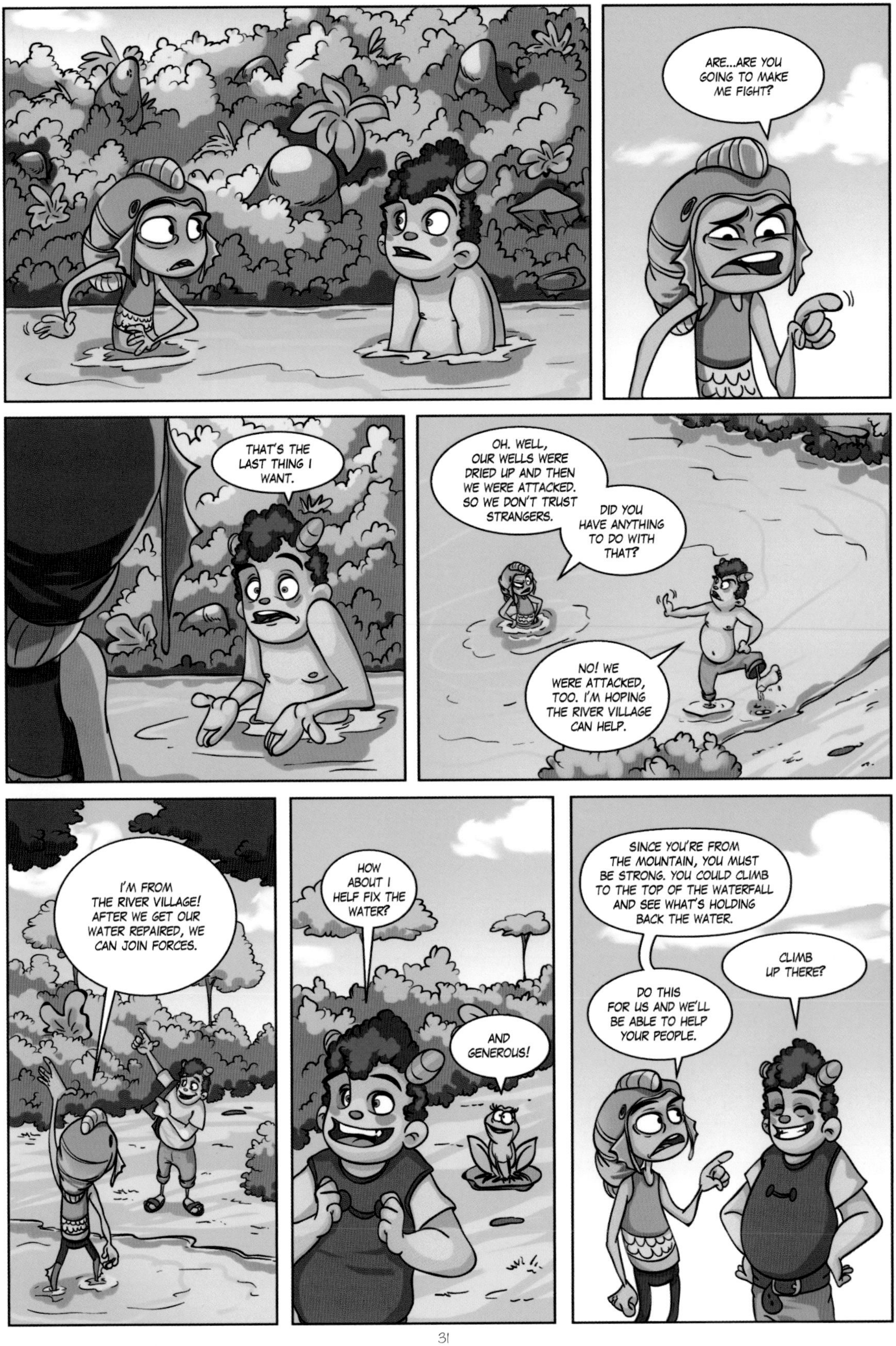
ARE...ARE YOU GOING TO MAKE ME FIGHT?
THAT'S THE LAST THING I WANT.
OH. WELL, OUR WELLS WERE DRIED UP AND THEN WE WERE ATTACKED. SO WE DON'T TRUST STRANGERS.
DID YOU HAVE ANYTHING TO DO WITH THAT?
NO! WE WERE ATTACKED, TOO. I'M HOPING THE RIVER VILLAGE CAN HELP.
I'M FROM THE RIVER VILLAGE! AFTER WE GET OUR WATER REPAIRED, WE CAN JOIN FORCES.
HOW ABOUT I HELF FIX THE WATER?
AND GENEROUS!
SINCE YOU'RE FROM THE MOUNTAIN, YOU MUST BE STRONG. YOU COULD CLIMB TO THE TOP OF THE WATERFALL AND SEE WHAT'S HOLDING BACK THE WATER.
DO THIS FOR US AND WE'LL BE ABLE TO HELP YOUR PEOPLE.
CLIMB UP THERE?

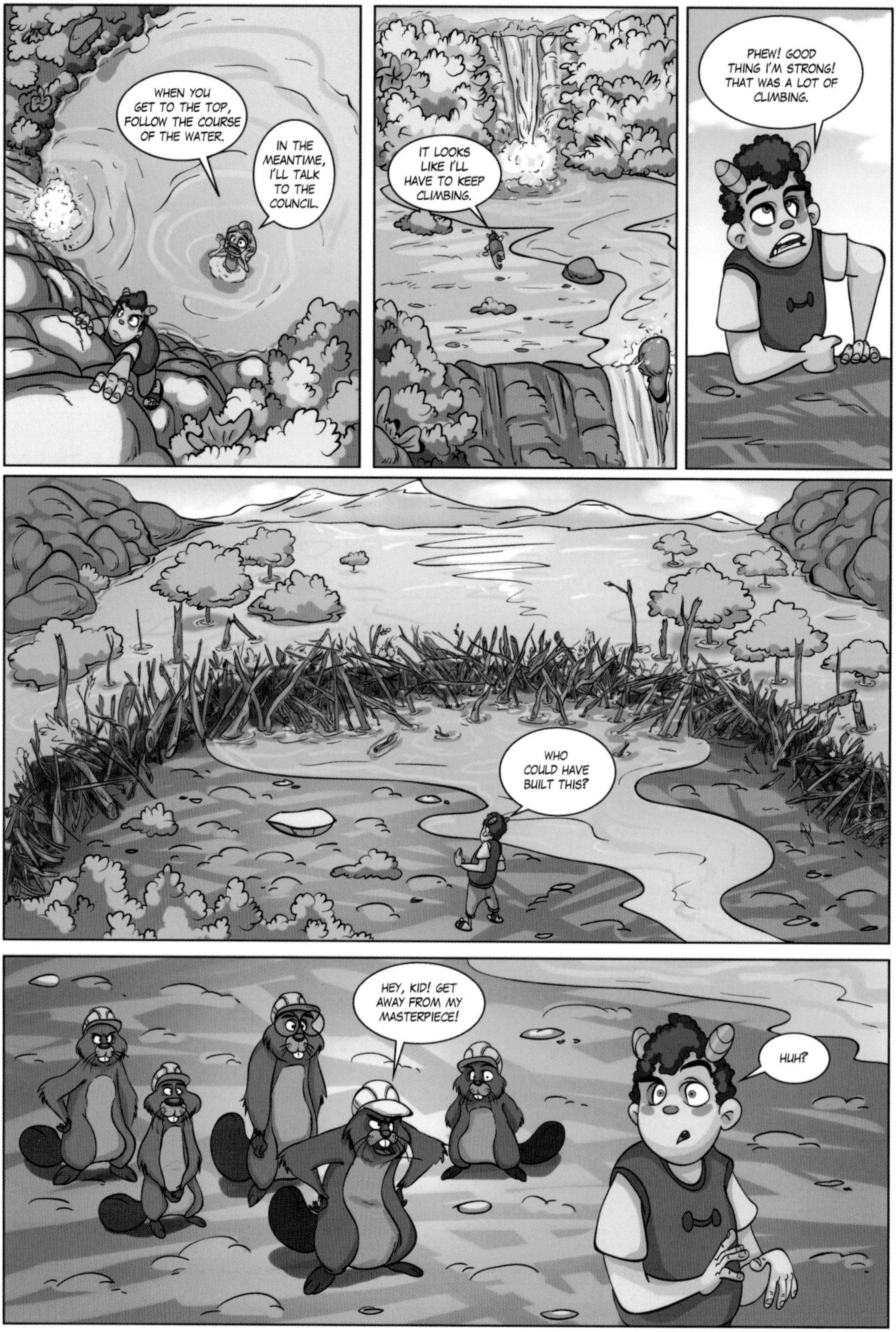
WHEN YOU GET TO THE TOP, FOLLOW THE COURSE OF THE WATER.
IN THE MEANTIME, I'LL TALK TO THE COUNCIL.
IT LOOKS LIKE I'LL HAVE TO KEEP CLIMBING.
PHEW! GOOD THING I'M STRONG! THAT WAS A LOT OF CLIMBING.
WHO COULD HAVE BUILT THIS?
HEY, KID! GET AWAY FROM MY MASTERPIECE!
HUH?

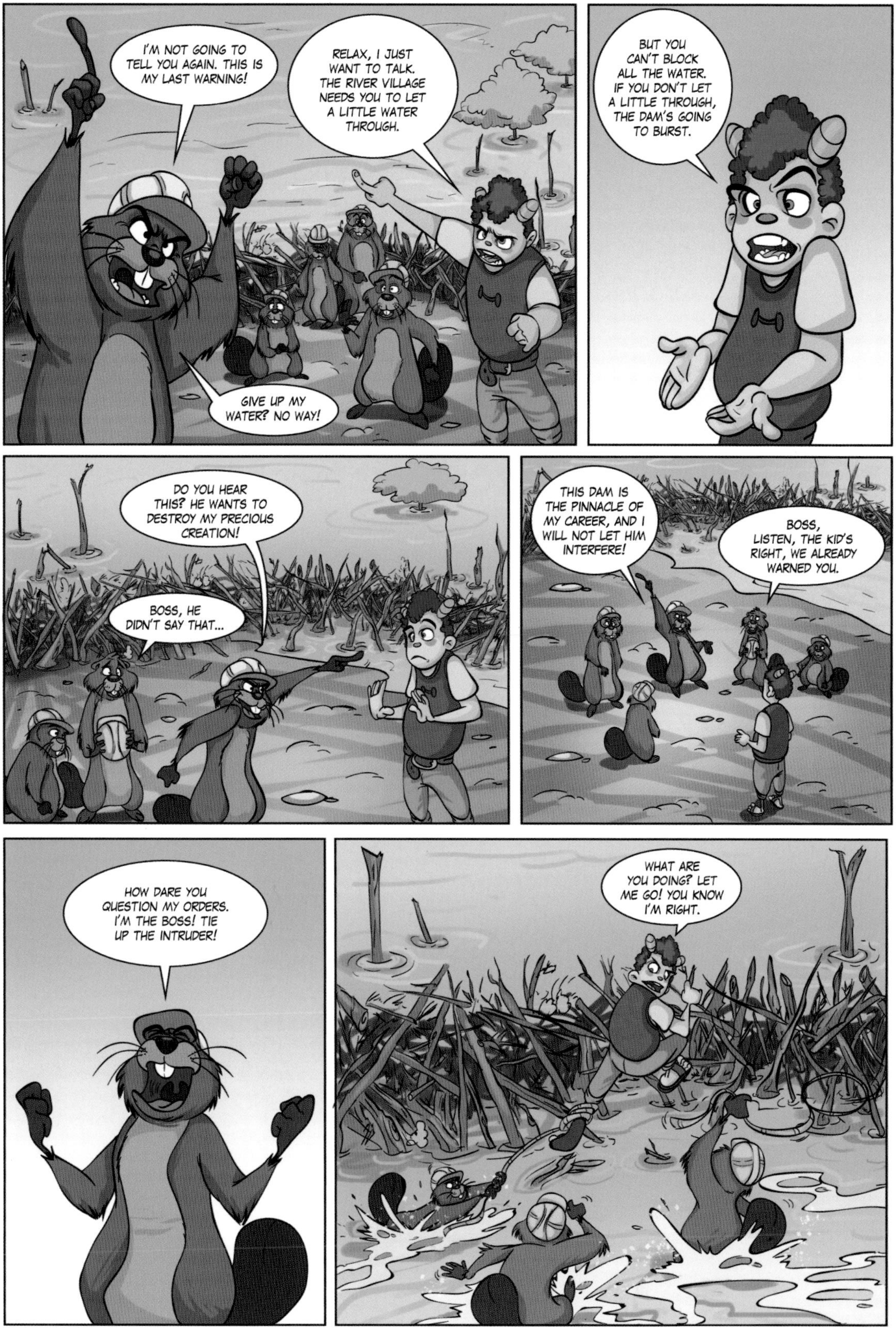
I'M NOT GOING TO TELL YOU AGAIN. THIS IS MY LAST WARNING!
RELAX, I JUST WANT TO TALK. THE RIVER VILLAGE NEEDS YOU TO LET A LITTLE WATER THROUGH.
GIVE UP MY WATER? NO WAY!
BUT YOU CAN'T BLOCK ALL THE WATER. IF YOU DON'T LET A LITTLE THROUGH, THE DAM'S GOING TO BURST.
DO YOU HEAR THIS? HE WANTS TO DESTROY MY PRECIOUS CREATION!
BOSS, HE DIDN'T SAY THAT...
THIS DAM IS THE PINNACLE OF MY CAREER, AND I WILL NOT LET HIM INTERFERE!
BOSS, LISTEN, THE KID'S RIGHT, WE ALREADY WARNED YOU.
HOW DARE YOU QUESTION MY ORDERS. I'M THE BOSS! TIE UP THE INTRUDER!
WHAT ARE YOU DOING? LET ME GO! YOU KNOW I'M RIGHT.

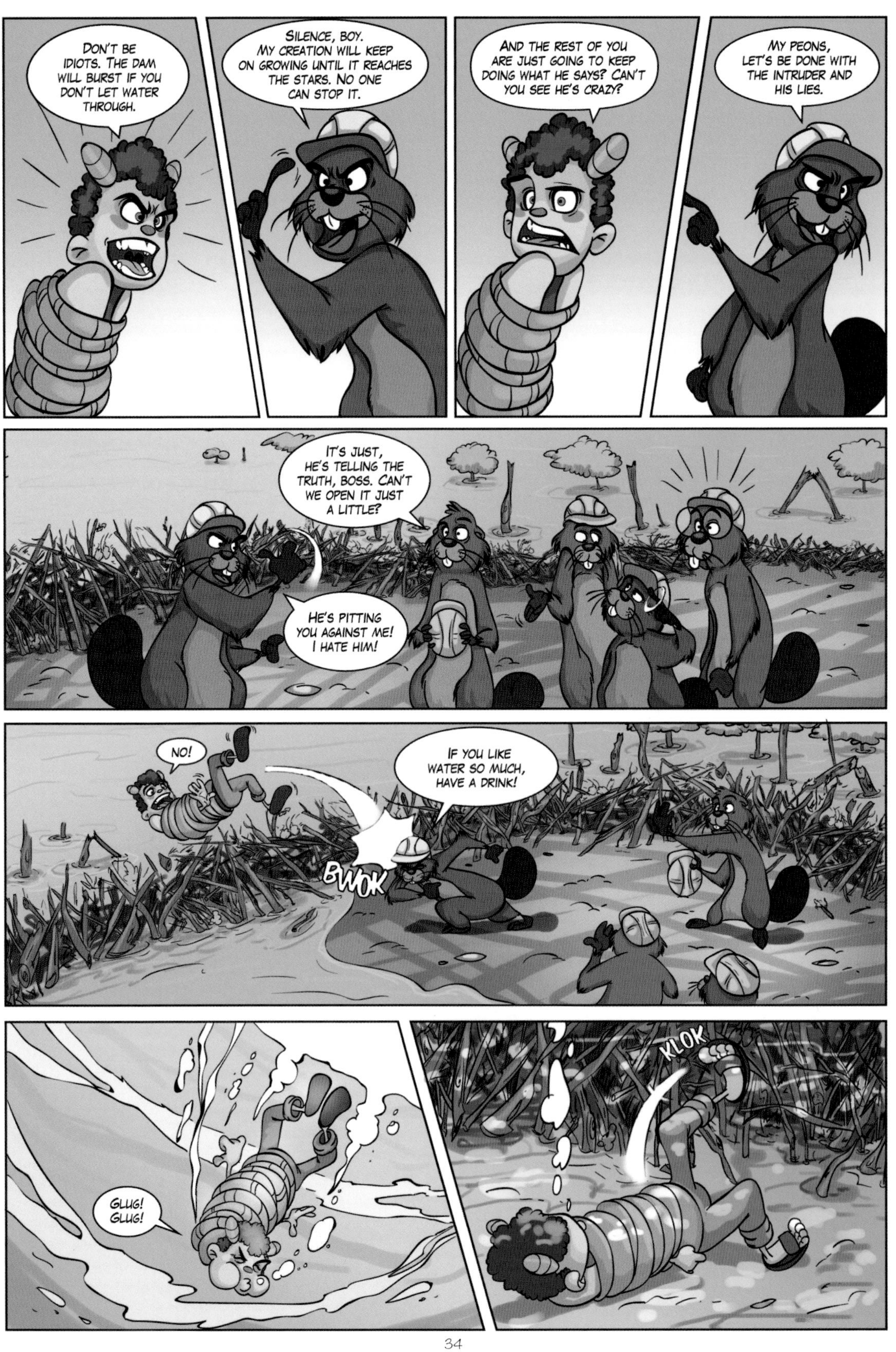
DON'T BE IDIOTS. THE DAM WILL BURST IF YOU DON'T LET WATER THROUGH.
SILENCE, BOY. MY CREATION WILL KEEP ON GROWING UNTIL IT REACHES THE STARS. NO ONE CAN STOP IT.
AND THE REST OF YOU ARE JUST GOING TO KEEP DOING WHAT HE SAYS? CAN'T YOU SEE HE'S CRAZY?
MY PEONS, LET'S BE DONE WITH THE INTRUDER AND HIS LIES.
IT'S JUST, HE'S TELLING THE TRUTH, BOSS. CAN'T WE OPEN IT JUST A LITTLE?
HE'S PITTING YOU AGAINST ME! I HATE HIM!
NO!
IF YOU LIKE WATER SO MUCH, HAVE A DRINK!
BWOK
GLUG! GLUG!
KLOK

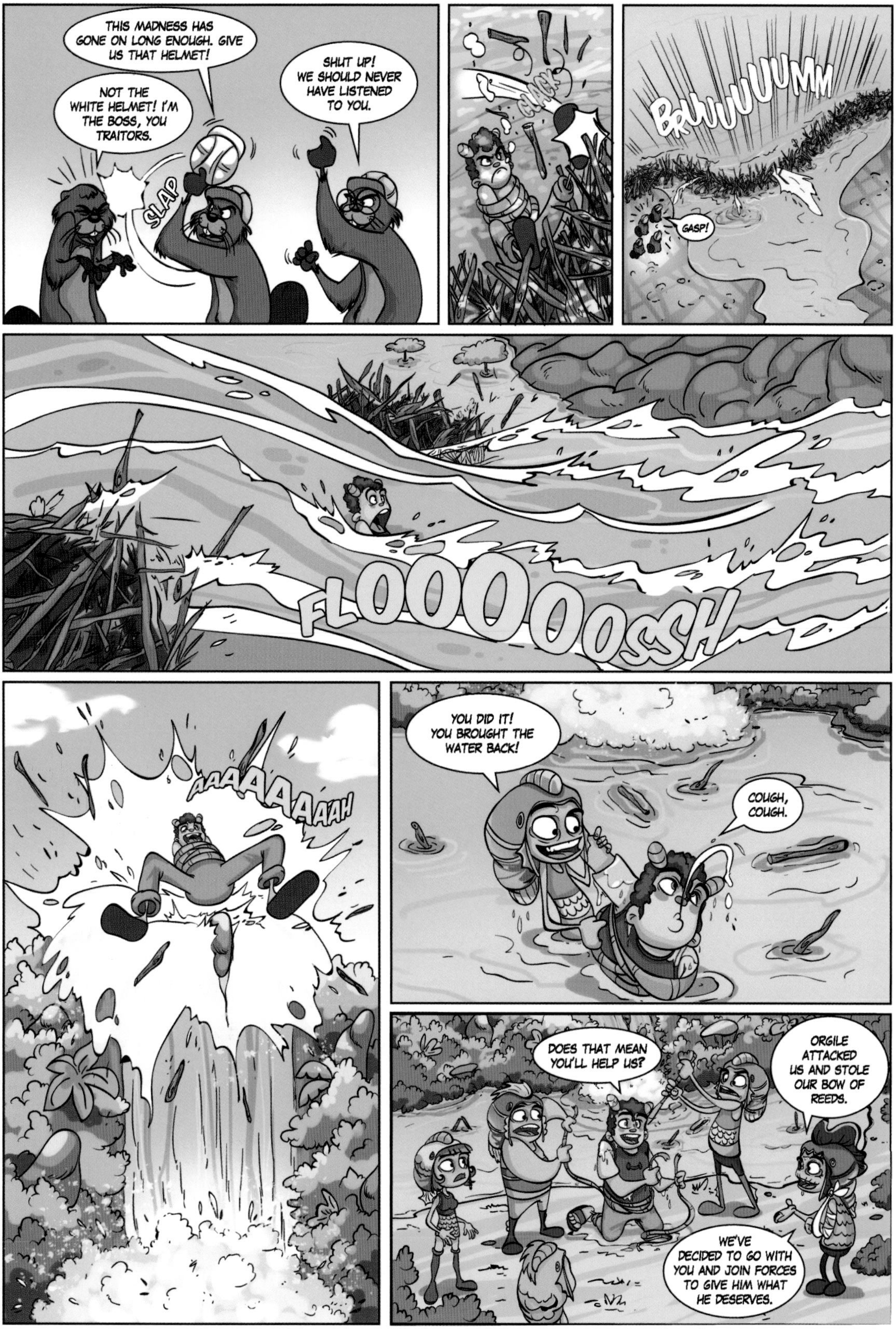
THIS MADNESS HAS GONE ON LONG ENOUGH. GIVE US THAT HELMET!
NOT THE WHITE HELMET! I'M THE BOSS, YOU TRAITORS.
SLAP
SHUT UP! WE SHOULD NEVER HAVE LISTENED TO YOU.
CLACK
BRUUUUUUMM
GASP!
FLOOOOOOSSH
AAAAAAAAAH
YOU DID IT! YOU BROUGHT THE WATER BACK!
COUGH, COUGH.
DOES THAT MEAN YOU'LL HELP US?
ORGILE ATTACKED US AND STOLE OUR BOW OF REEDS.
WE'VE DECIDED TO GO WITH YOU AND JOIN FORCES TO GIVE HIM WHAT HE DESERVES.

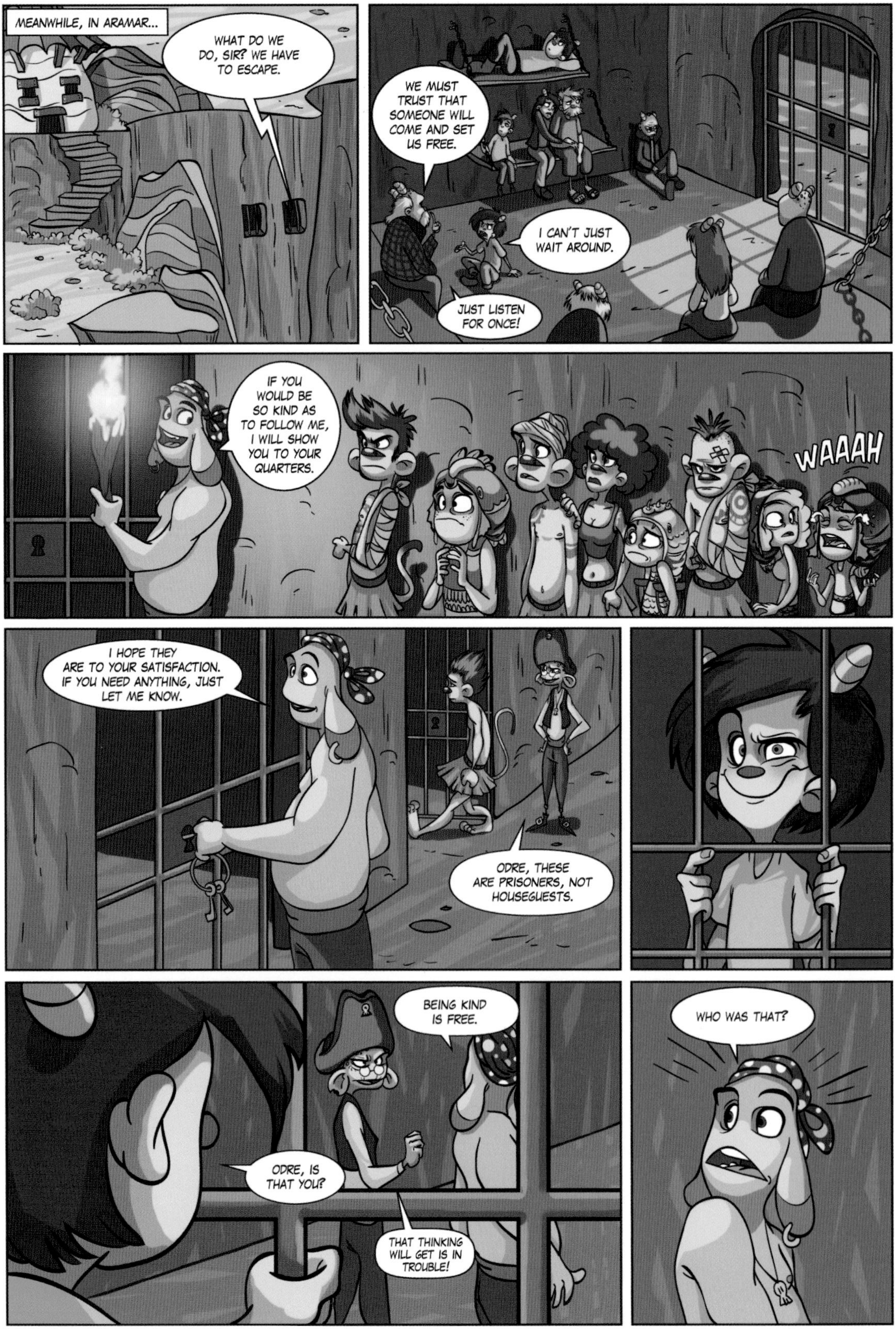
MEANWHILE, IN ARAMAR...
WHAT DO WE DO, SIR? WE HAVE TO ESCAPE.
WE MUST TRUST THAT SOMEONE WILL COME AND SET US FREE.
I CAN'T JUST WAIT AROUND.
JUST LISTEN FOR ONCE!
IF YOU WOULD BE SO KIND AS TO FOLLOW ME, I WILL SHOW YOU TO YOUR QUARTERS.
WAAAH
I HOPE THEY ARE TO YOUR SATISFACTION. IF YOU NEED ANYTHING, JUST LET ME KNOW.
ODRE, THESE ARE PRISONERS, NOT HOUSEGUESTS.
BEING KIND IS FREE.
ODRE, IS THAT YOU?
THAT THINKING WILL GET IS IN TROUBLE!
WHO WAS THAT?

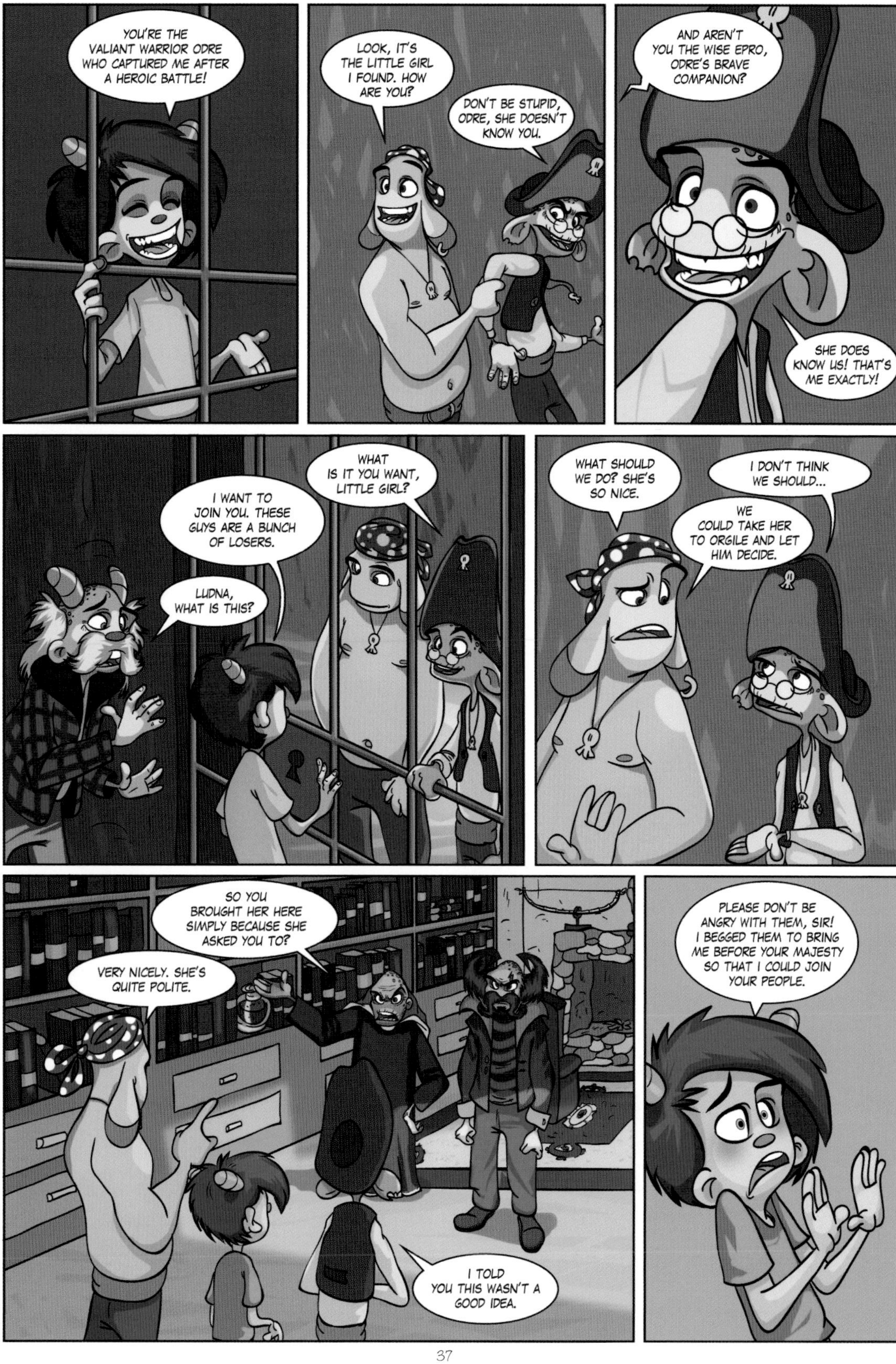

YOU'RE THE VALIANT WARRIOR ODRE WHO CAPTURED ME AFTER A HEROIC BATTLE!
LOOK, IT'S THE LITTLE GIRL I FOUND. HOW ARE YOU?
DON'T BE STUPID, ODRE, SHE DOESN'T KNOW YOU.
AND AREN'T YOU THE WISE EPRO, ODRE'S BRAVE COMPANION?
SHE DOES KNOW US! THAT'S ME EXACTLY!
LUDNA, WHAT IS THIS?
I WANT TO JOIN YOU. THESE GUYS ARE A BUNCH OF LOSERS.
WHAT IS IT YOU WANT, LITTLE GIRL?
WHAT SHOULD WE DO? SHE'S SO NICE.
I DON'T THINK WE SHOULD...
WE COULD TAKE HER TO ORGILE AND LET HIM DECIDE.
SO YOU BROUGHT HER HERE SIMPLY BECAUSE SHE ASKED YOU TO?
VERY NICELY. SHE'S QUITE POLITE.
I TOLD YOU THIS WASN'T A GOOD IDEA.
PLEASE DON'T BE ANGRY WITH THEM, SIR! I BEGGED THEM TO BRING ME BEFORE YOUR MAJESTY SO THAT I COULD JOIN YOUR PEOPLE.

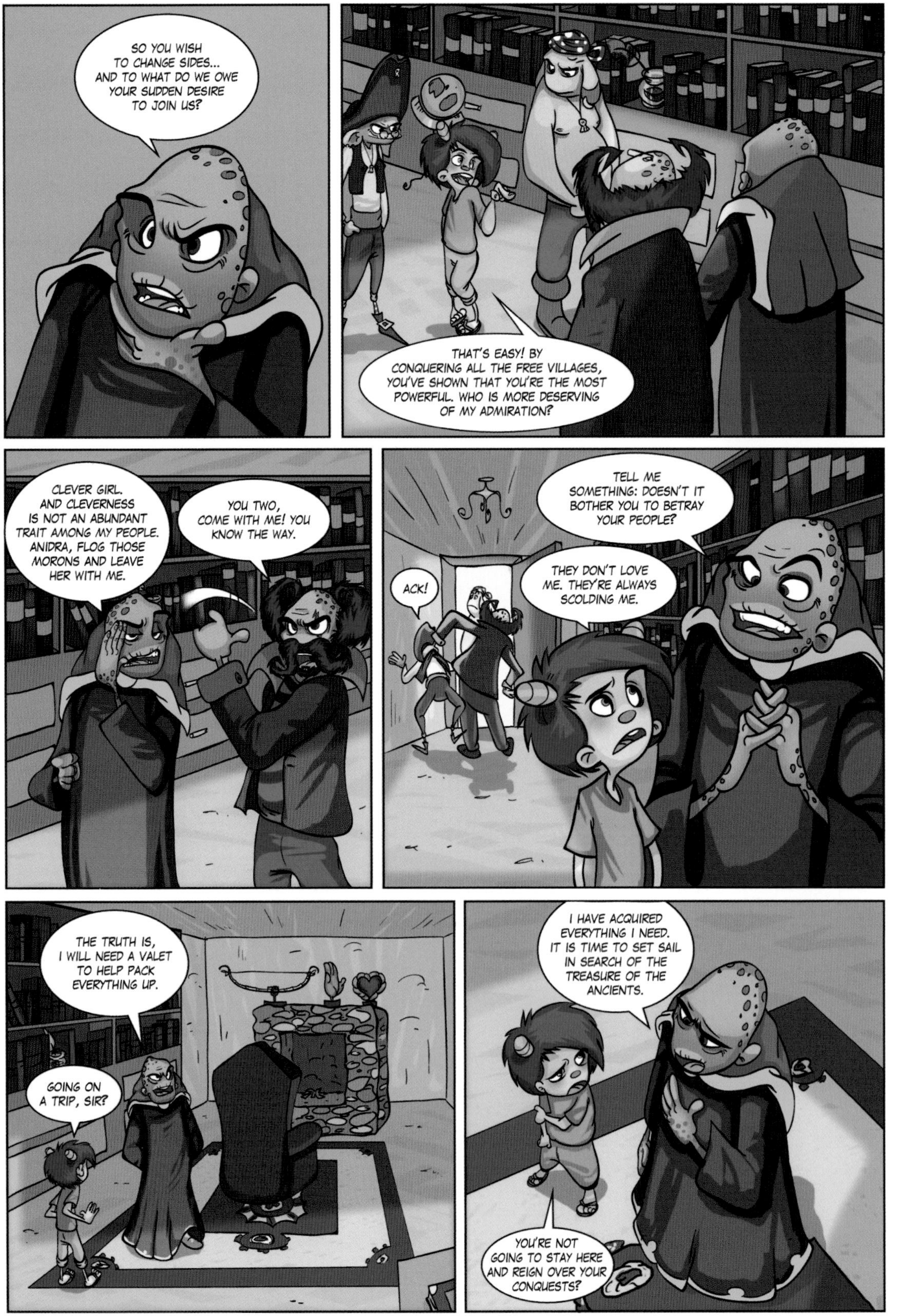
SO YOU WISH TO CHANGE SIDES... AND TO WHAT DO WE OWE YOUR SUDDEN DESIRE TO JOIN US?
THAT'S EASY! BY CONQUERING ALL THE FREE VILLAGES, YOU'VE SHOWN THAT YOU'RE THE MOST POWERFUL. WHO IS MORE DESERVING OF MY ADMIRATION?
CLEVER GIRL. AND CLEVERNESS IS NOT AN ABUNDANT TRAIT AMONG MY PEOPLE. ANIDRA, FLOG THOSE MORONS AND LEAVE HER WITH ME.
YOU TWO, COME WITH ME! YOU KNOW THE WAY.
ACK!
TELL ME SOMETHING: DOESN'T IT BOTHER YOU TO BETRAY YOUR PEOPLE?
THEY DON'T LOVE ME. THEY'RE ALWAYS SCOLDING ME.
THE TRUTH IS, I WILL NEED A VALET TO HELP PACK EVERYTHING UP.
GOING ON A TRIP, SIR?
I HAVE ACQUIRED EVERYTHING I NEED. IT IS TIME TO SET SAIL IN SEARCH OF THE TREASURE OF THE ANCIENTS.
YOU'RE NOT GOING TO STAY HERE AND REIGN OVER YOUR CONQUESTS?

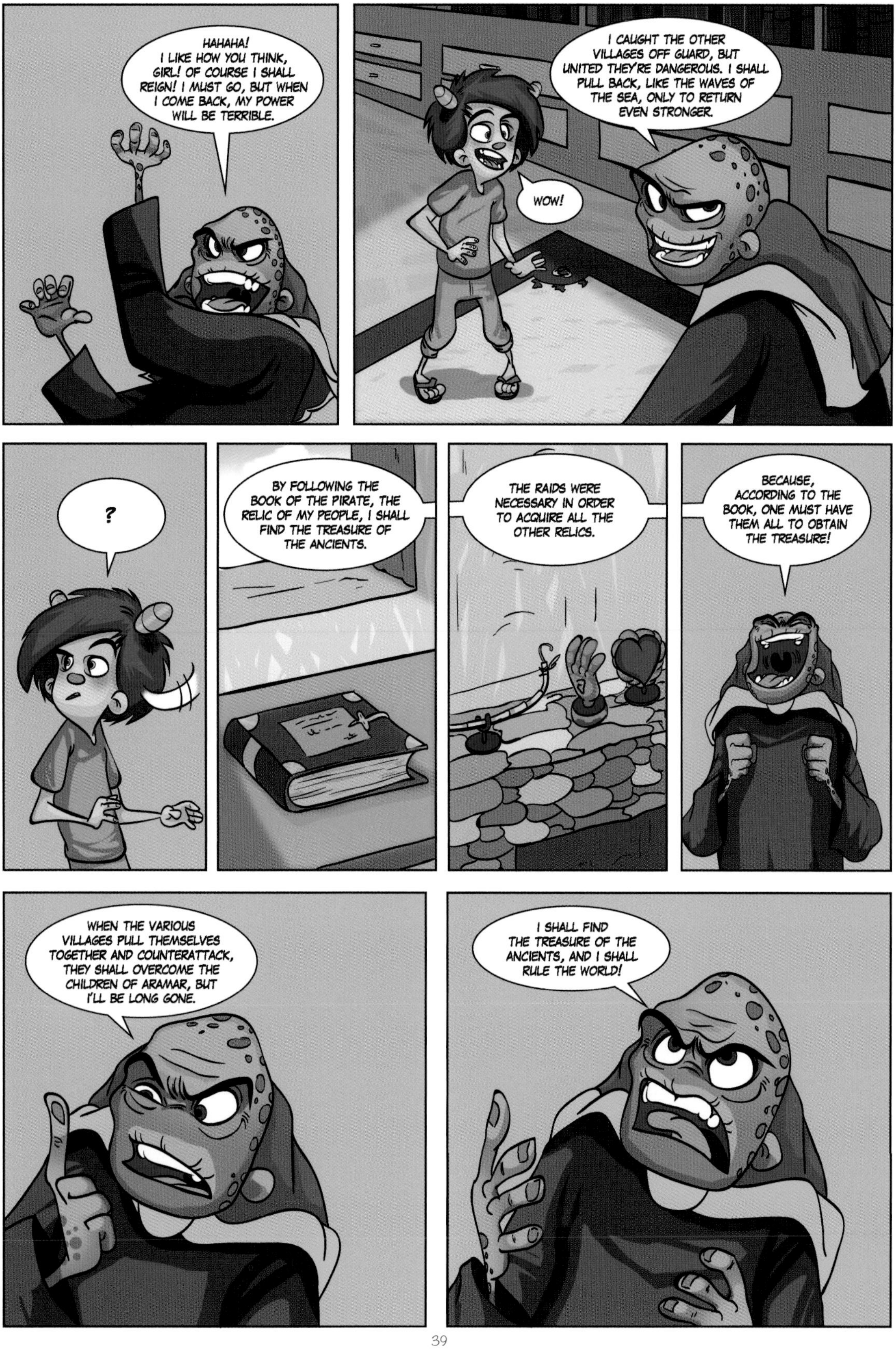

HAHAHA! I LIKE HOW YOU THINK, GIRL! OF COURSE I SHALL REIGN! I MUST GO, BUT WHEN I COME BACK, MY POWER WILL BE TERRIBLE.
I CAUGHT THE OTHER VILLAGES OFF GUARD, BUT UNITED THEY'RE DANGEROUS. I SHALL PULL BACK, LIKE THE WAVES OF THE SEA, ONLY TO RETURN EVEN STRONGER.
WOW!
?
BY FOLLOWING THE BOOK OF THE PIRATE, THE RELIC OF MY PEOPLE, I SHALL FIND THE TREASURE OF THE ANCIENTS.
THE RAIDS WERE NECESSARY IN ORDER TO ACQUIRE ALL THE OTHER RELICS.
BECAUSE, ACCORDING TO THE BOOK, ONE MUST HAVE THEM ALL TO OBTAIN THE TREASURE!
WHEN THE VARIOUS VILLAGES PULL THEMSELVES TOGETHER AND COUNTERATTACK, THEY SHALL OVERCOME THE CHILDREN OF ARAMAR, BUT I'LL BE LONG GONE.
I SHALL FIND THE TREASURE OF THE ANCIENTS, AND I SHALL RULE THE WORLD!

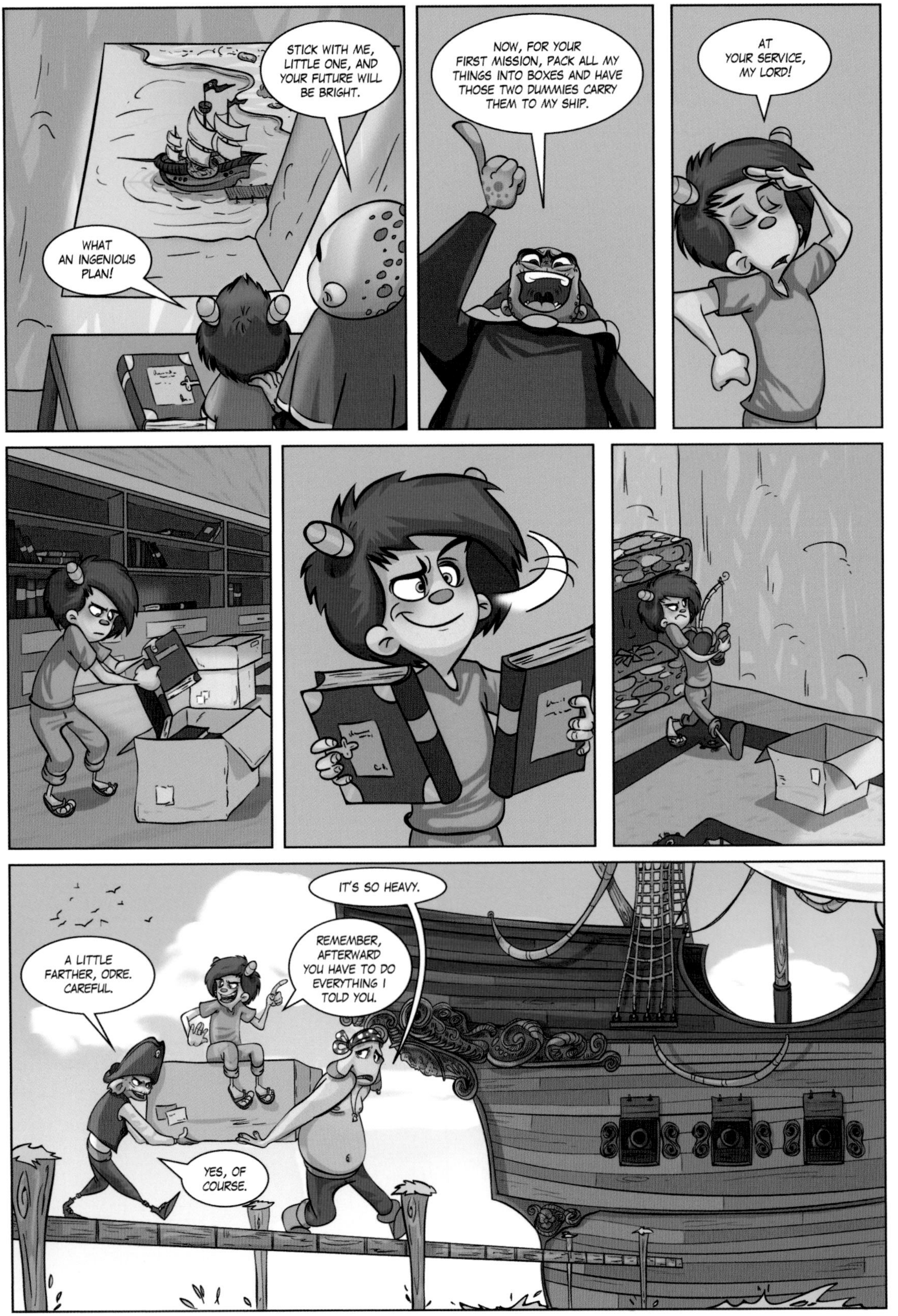
STICK WITH ME, LITTLE ONE, AND YOUR FUTURE WILL BE BRIGHT.
WHAT AN INGENIOUS PLAN!
NOW, FOR YOUR FIRST MISSION, PACK ALL MY THINGS INTO BOXES AND HAVE THOSE TWO DUMMIES CARRY THEM TO MY SHIP.
AT YOUR SERVICE, MY LORD!
IT'S SO HEAVY.
A LITTLE FARTHER, ODRE. CAREFUL.
REMEMBER, AFTERWARD YOU HAVE TO DO EVERYTHING I TOLD YOU.
YES, OF COURSE.

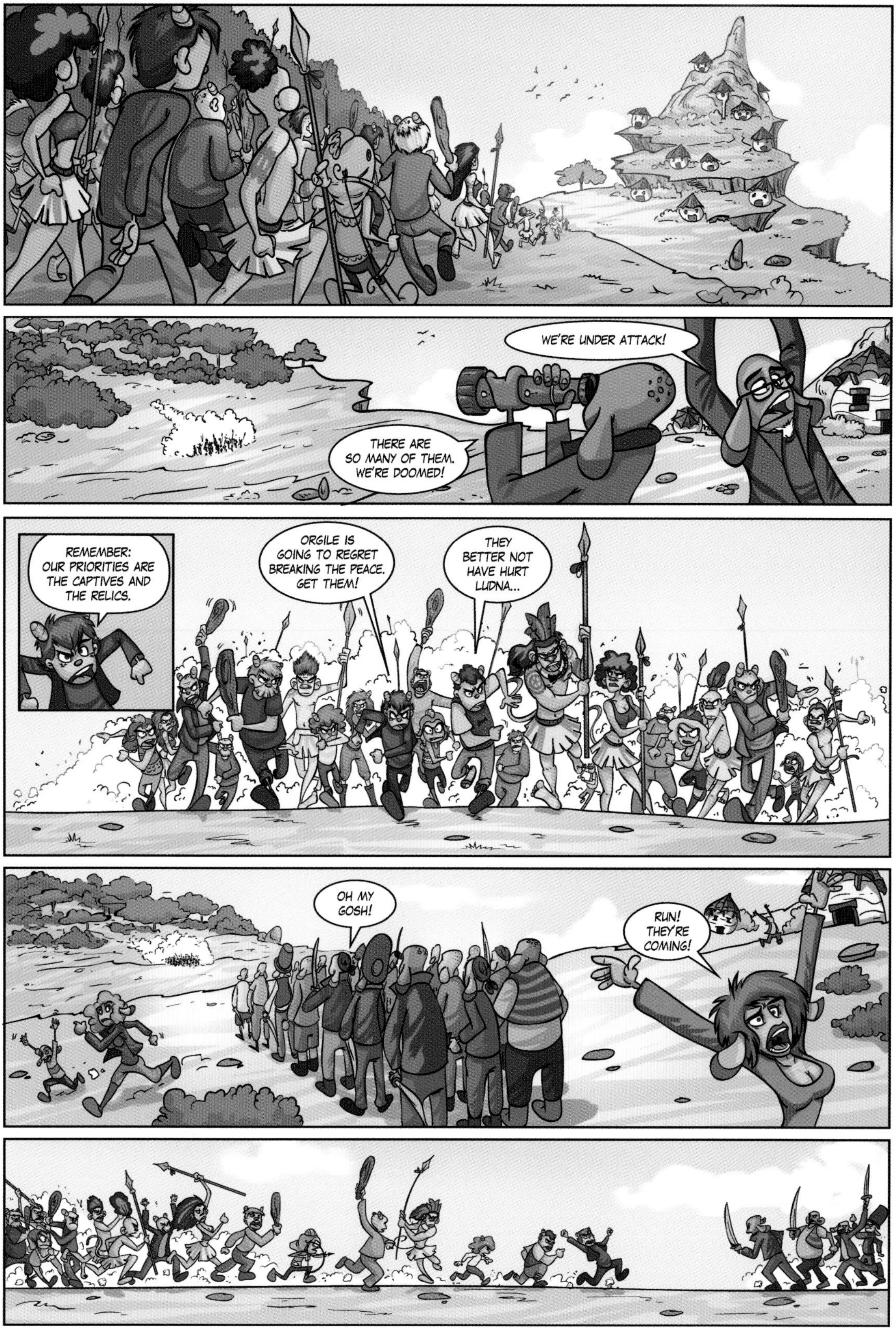
WE'RE UNDER ATTACK!
THERE ARE SO MANY OF THEM. WE'RE DOOMED!
REMEMBER: OUR PRIORITIES ARE THE CAPTIVES AND THE RELICS.
ORGILE IS GOING TO REGRET BREAKING THE PEACE. GET THEM!
THEY BETTER NOT HAVE HURT LUDNA...
OH MY GOSH!
RUN! THEY'RE COMING!

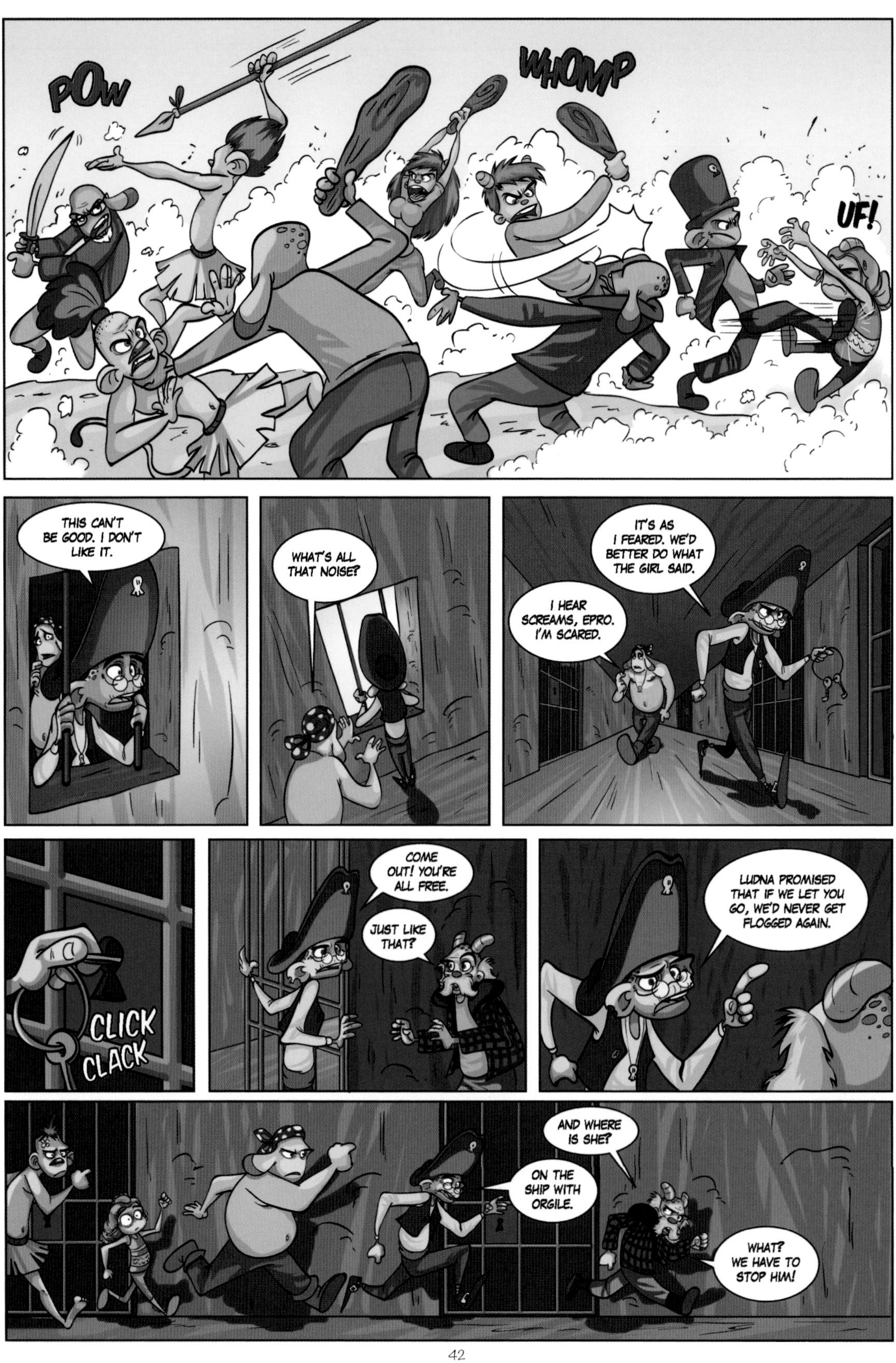
POW
WHOMP
UF!
THIS CAN'T BE GOOD. I DON'T LIKE IT.
WHAT'S ALL THAT NOISE?
IT'S AS I FEARED. WE'D BETTER DO WHAT THE GIRL SAID.
I HEAR SCREAMS, EPRO. I'M SCARED.
CLICK
CLACK
COME OUT! YOU'RE ALL FREE.
JUST LIKE THAT?
LUDNA PROMISED THAT IF WE LET YOU GO, WE'D NEVER GET FLOGGED AGAIN.
AND WHERE IS SHE?
ON THE SHIP WITH ORGILE.
WHAT? WE HAVE TO STOP HIM!

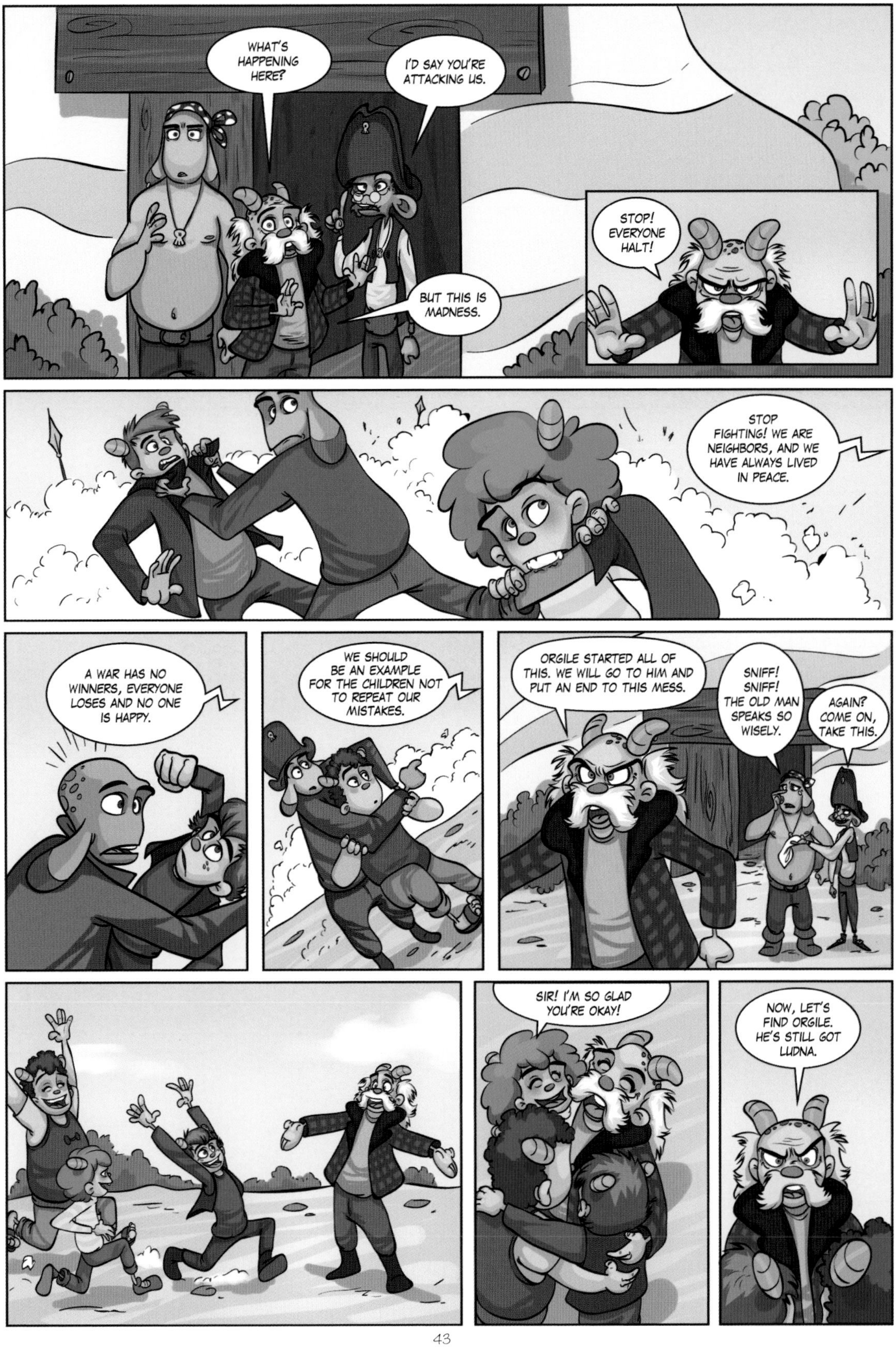
WHAT'S HAPPENING HERE?
I'D SAY YOU'RE ATTACKING US.
BUT THIS IS MADNESS.
STOP! EVERYONE HALT!
STOP FIGHTING! WE ARE NEIGHBORS, AND WE HAVE ALWAYS LIVED IN PEACE.
A WAR HAS NO WINNERS, EVERYONE LOSES AND NO ONE IS HAPPY.
WE SHOULD BE AN EXAMPLE FOR THE CHILDREN NOT TO REPEAT OUR MISTAKES.
ORGILE STARTED ALL OF THIS. WE WILL GO TO HIM AND PUT AN END TO THIS MESS.
SNIFF! SNIFF! THE OLD MAN SPEAKS SO WISELY.
AGAIN? COME ON, TAKE THIS.
SIR! I'M SO GLAD YOU'RE OKAY!
NOW, LET'S FIND ORGILE. HE'S STILL GOT LUDNA.

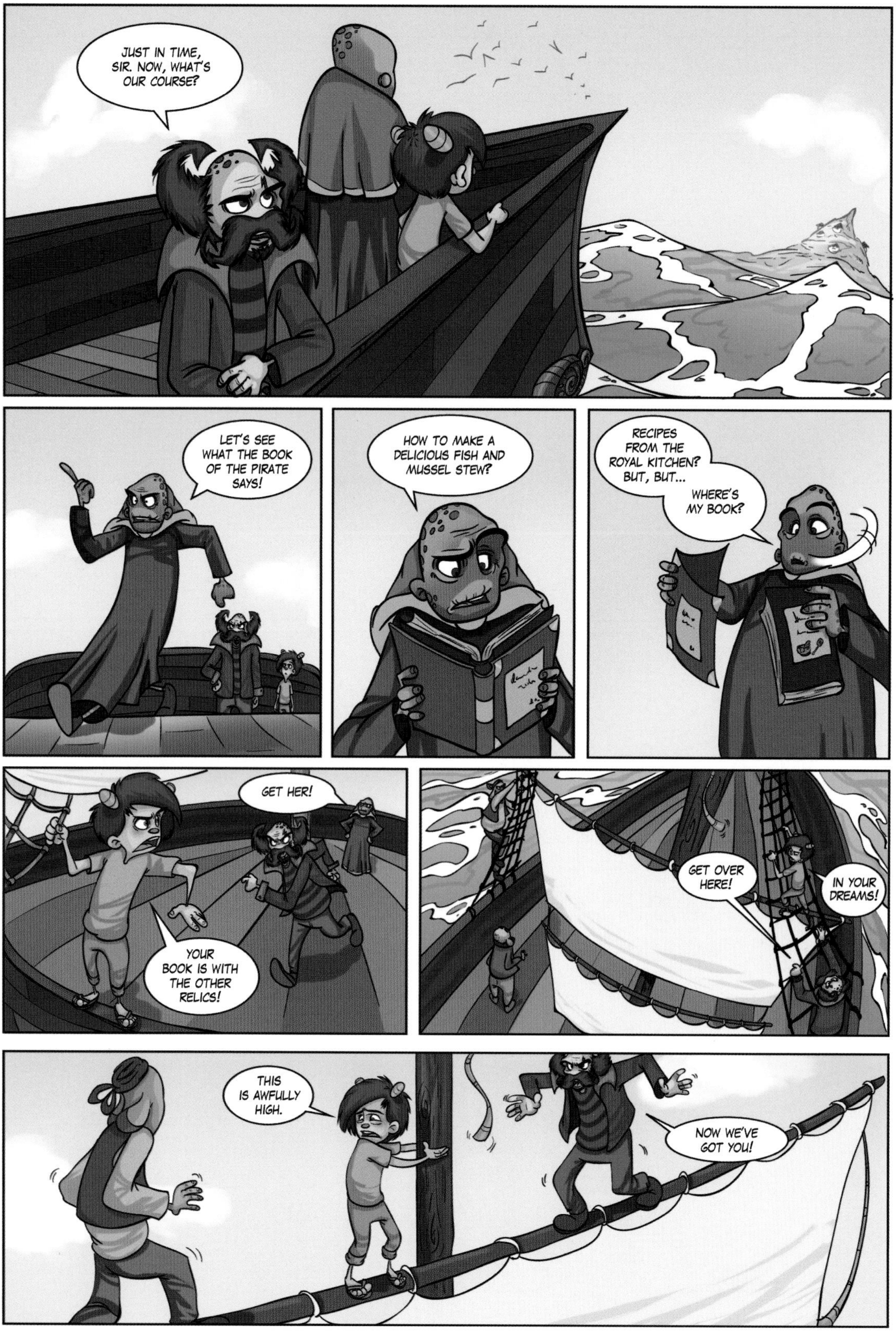
JUST IN TIME, SIR. NOW, WHAT'S OUR COURSE?
LET'S SEE WHAT THE BOOK OF THE PIRATE SAYS!
HOW TO MAKE A DELICIOUS FISH AND MUSSEL STEW?
RECIPES FROM THE ROYAL KITCHEN? BUT, BUT...
WHERE'S MY BOOK?
GET HER!
YOUR BOOK IS WITH THE OTHER RELICS!
GET OVER HERE!
IN YOUR DREAMS!
THIS IS AWFULLY HIGH.
NOW WE'VE GOT YOU!

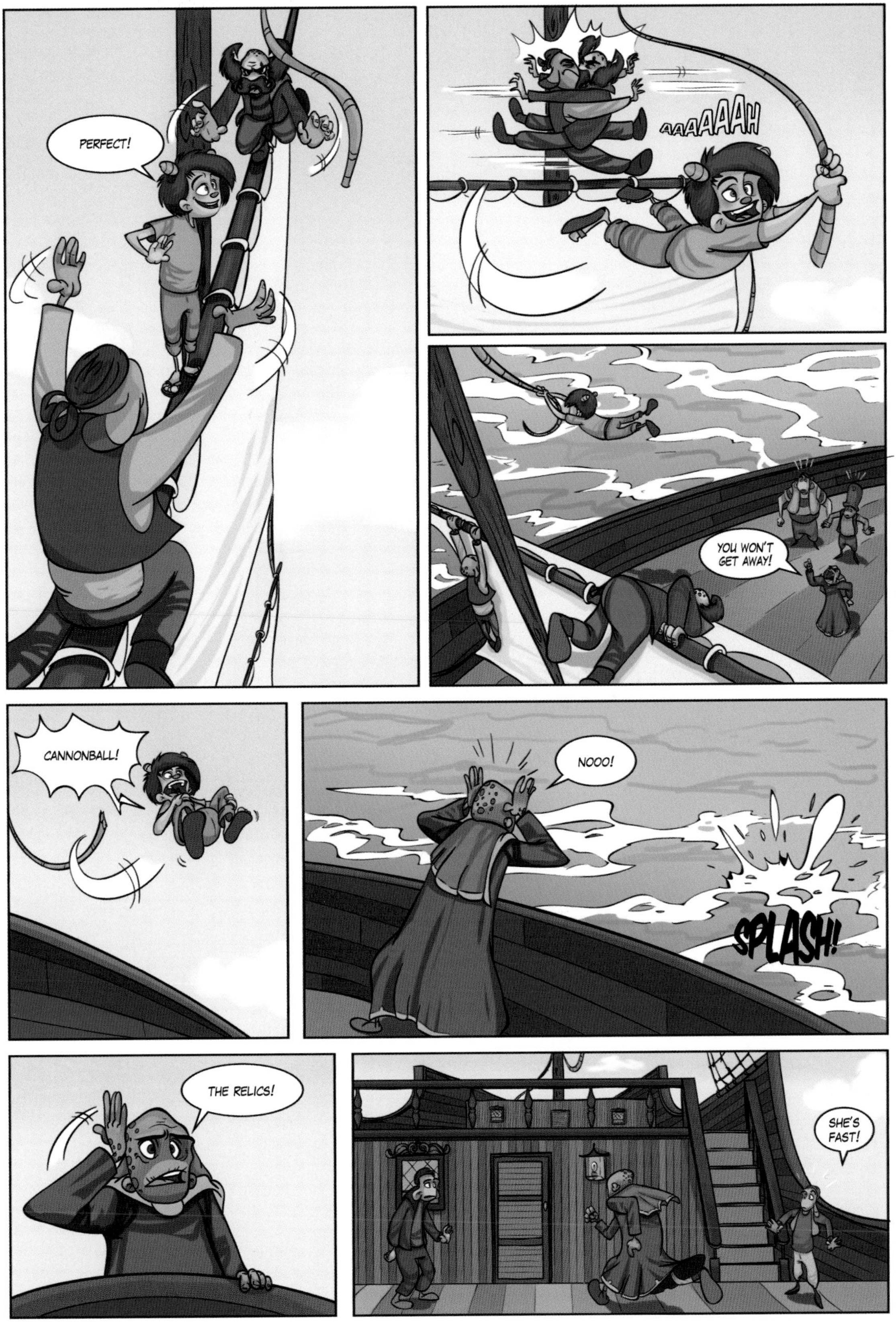
PERFECT!
AAAAAAH
YOU WON'T GET AWAY!
CANNONBALL!
NOOO!
SPLASH!
THE RELICS!
SHE'S FAST!

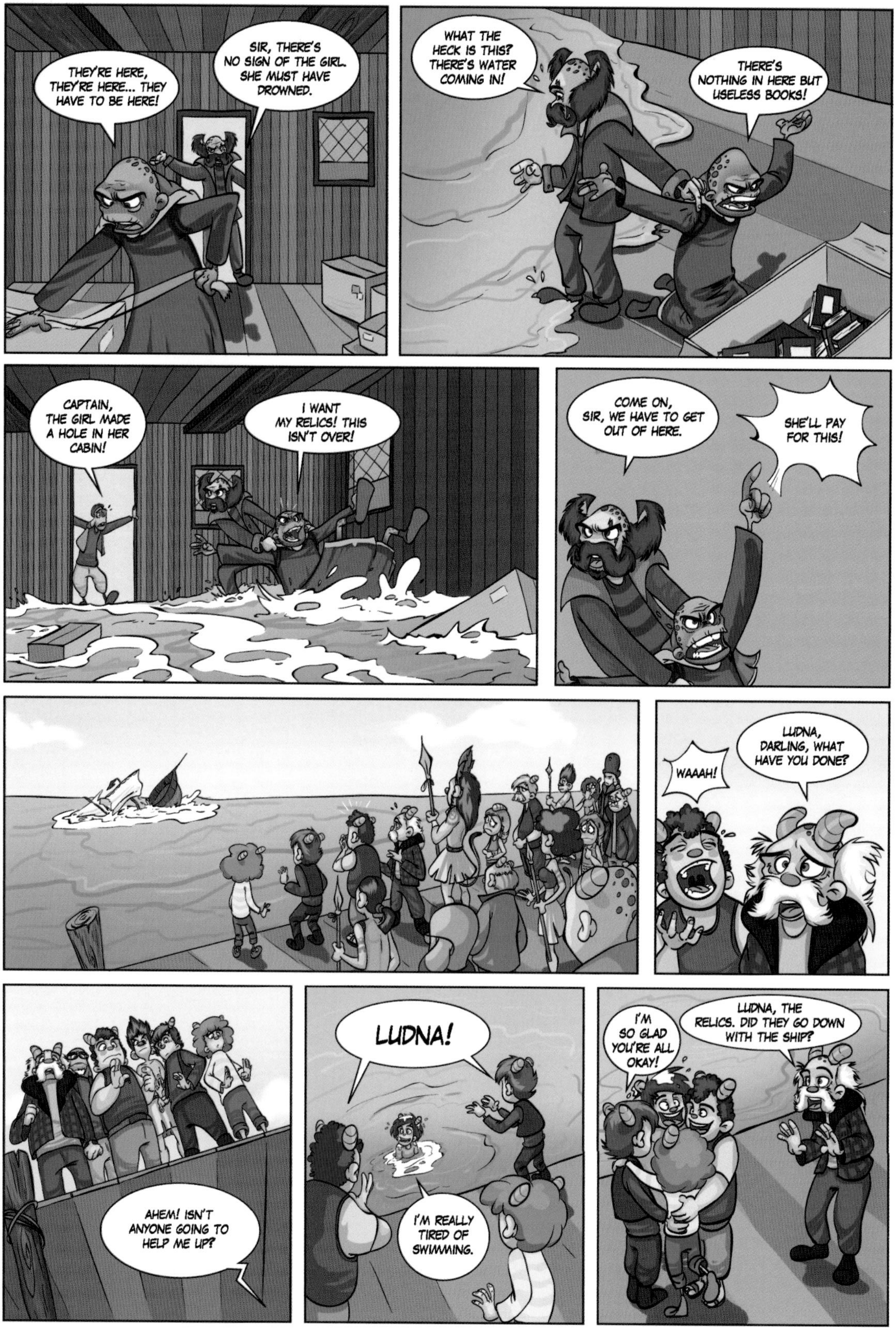
THEY'RE HERE, THEY'RE HERE... THEY HAVE TO BE HERE!
SIR, THERE'S NO SIGN OF THE GIRL. SHE MUST HAVE DROWNED.
WHAT THE HECK IS THIS? THERE'S WATER COMING IN!
THERE'S NOTHING IN HERE BUT USELESS BOOKS!
CAPTAIN, THE GIRL MADE A HOLE IN HER CABIN!
I WANT MY RELICS! THIS ISN'T OVER!
COME ON, SIR, WE HAVE TO GET OUT OF HERE.
SHE'LL PAY FOR THIS!
WAAAH!
LUDNA, DARLING, WHAT HAVE YOU DONE?
AHEM! ISN'T ANYONE GOING TO HELP ME UP?
LUDNA!
I'M REALLY TIRED OF SWIMMING.
I'M SO GLAD YOU'RE ALL OKAY!
LUDNA, THE RELICS. DID THEY GO DOWN WITH THE SHIP?

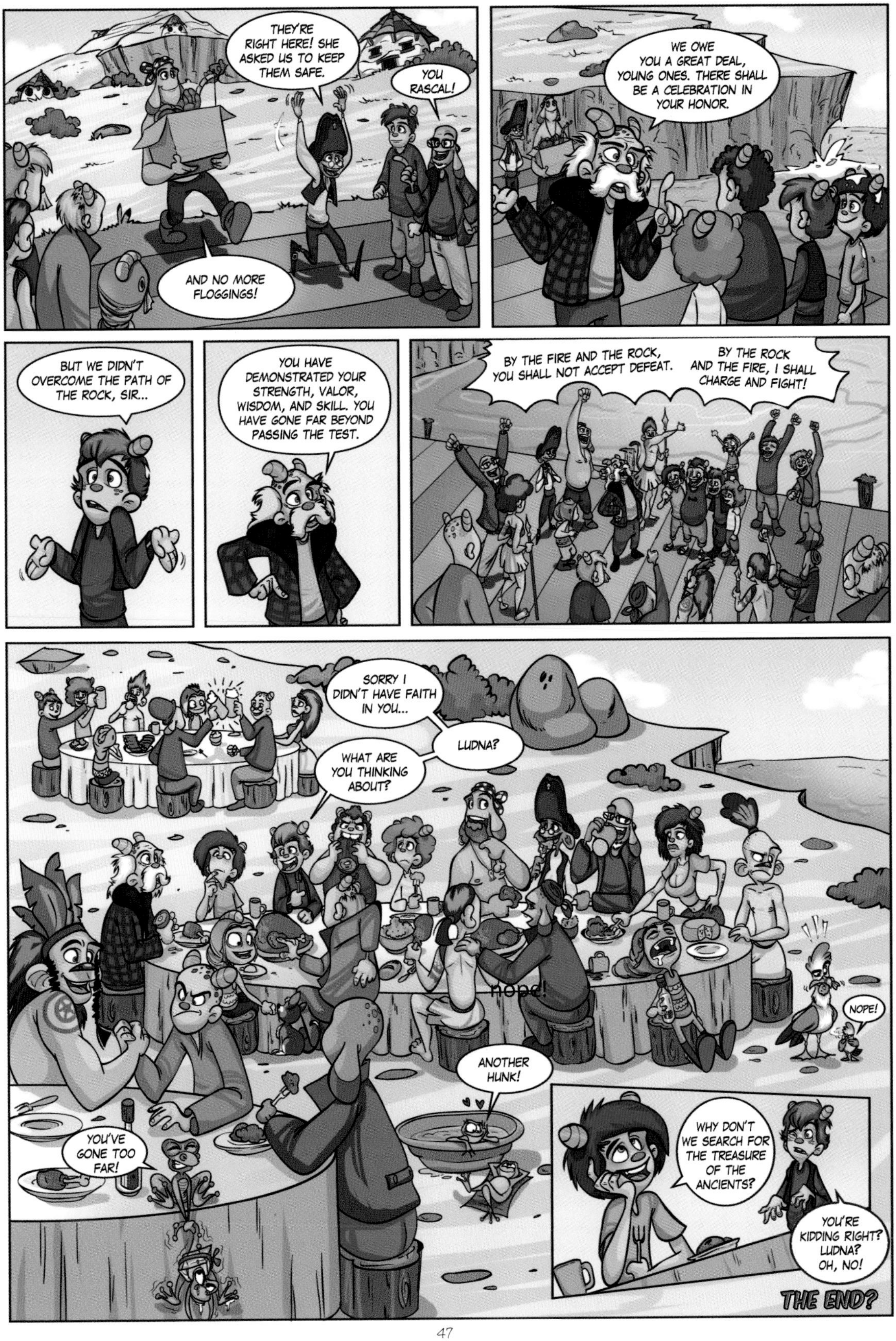
THEY'RE RIGHT HERE! SHE ASKED US TO KEEP THEM SAFE.
YOU RASCAL!
AND NO MORE FLOGGINGS!
WE OWE YOU A GREAT DEAL, YOUNG ONES. THERE SHALL BE A CELEBRATION IN YOUR HONOR.
BUT WE DIDN'T OVERCOME THE PATH OF THE ROCK, SIR...
YOU HAVE DEMONSTRATED YOUR STRENGTH, VALOR, WISDOM, AND SKILL. YOU HAVE GONE FAR BEYOND PASSING THE TEST.
BY THE FIRE AND THE ROCK, YOU SHALL NOT ACCEPT DEFEAT.
BY THE ROCK AND THE FIRE, I SHALL CHARGE AND FIGHT!
SORRY I DIDN'T HAVE FAITH IN YOU...
LUDNA?
WHAT ARE YOU THINKING ABOUT?
nope!
NOPE!
ANOTHER HUNK!
YOU'VE GONE TOO FAR!
WHY DON'T WE SEARCH FOR THE TREASURE OF THE ANCIENTS?
YOU'RE KIDDING RIGHT? LUDNA? OH, NO!
THE END?